DANGEROUS HAVEN

KAREN L. ABRAHAMSON

GET KAREN L. ABRAHAMSON'S ROMANCE STARTER KIT…

Sign up for the no-spam newsletter and receive a three
novels/novellas and lots more content—all free!
Details can be found at the end of *Dangerous Haven*.

DANGEROUS HAVEN

Karen L. Abrahamson

PROLOGUE

Kindled by the anguish of damned souls, the Underworld's sky burned bright overhead. Sisyphus strained in the sweltering air. Sweat poured down his body and his muscles bulged as he rolled the huge white granite boulder another few feet. More sweat stung his eyes and dripped from his ragged black hair and beard. His bare toes clutched and dug a deep trough underfoot. It looked as if his path had been traveled by many feet, but his alone had gouged the earth and stone of the hill over the centuries. Back and forth. Up and down this damned hillside until he thought he might go mad at the futility. Always he had been a driven man—to get what he wanted. What he needed. If others stood in the way of his goal, he dealt with them.

He had thought that was what all men did.

Apparently,he had been wrong, for there were no other men wrestling this damned boulder with him. After all these years, Hades, King of the Underworld, had still not taken pity on him. Couldn't the god realize that Sisyphus was a man, flawed like all men?

The fiery sky shimmered—no sun, simply a searing, incandescent glow that eternally filled the heavens. His shoulders screamed, just as they had for three thousand years of penance and just as, through every second of those three thousand years, he had thought that he could not go on. Sulfur and brimstone weighted the air and left him gasping. Just a few more feet and he would reach the top of the two-hundred-foot hill. A few more feet and the stone could rest in the indentation there and he could rest from his labors and enjoy the view of the netherworld. In his struggles up the hill and in his tumbles down to the bottom, he had caught glimpses of the broad plain of Hell. Far away there were flames shooting up to the sky, and in the other direction, the broad, dark river was surely the Styx beyond which was life and his country.

His country. What had his fool son done to it in his absence… The land, the creatures that inhabited it—that was the eternal part. But countries?

No. His son had likely carried on after his father, and like his father, he had done the best he could while he lived. He would be long dead and dust by now. Men were born and spent themselves on worldly pursuits, but the land continued. It alone had a true purpose of sustaining life.

It was the first time, after all these years of bitterness, that he had realized such a thing. It mattered not what a man did as long as he left the land no worse off than it had been. Countries, kingdoms, and empires rose and fell. Over time, they meant nothing.

It was something to think about on the next hard journey up the hill. And the next. And the next. He held his shoulder against the stone, straining with his arms to stop it from falling back and crushing him as it had done so many times when he had first been set on this hill. Over the millennia his muscles had increased, but so had the size of the massive boulder, as if Hades wished him to always use maximum effort in this futile task.

He dug in his toes, used his thighs to lever himself and the weight of the stone higher.

It rolled—a little.

He shoved again, keeping up the momentum. Another step, his shoulder against the granite, and the boulder inched its way closer to the top of the hill. Every time he reached the hill's crown there came a crash of lightning and thunder,and the roar of the thunder threw him down and sent him and the boulder tumbling down the hill to the bottom.

To begin the long labor again.

Once, early on, he had tried to refuse the labor. He'd found himself in the path of the boulder and been crushed to death. He'd woken once more on the hillside with his shoulder pressed against granite. He'd been crushed again for his refusal, only this time he'd been allowed to live crushed and broken until he had agreed to pick up this task.

The boulder wobbled on the lip of the hilltop. Overhead the glowing sky darkened. He held his breath. His cheek and chin were pressed against the granite that had long ago become stained dark brown from the blood of his hands.

But there was no spike of lightning. No crash of thunder. He gave another mighty push and the boulder trembled—and then rolled down away from him to settle into the divot in the center of the dirt and ashes of the hilltop. For the first time in millennia, Sisyphus straightened.

He worked his shoulders.

How long had it been since he had stood upright without the weight of the boulder against his shoulders? He felt strangely naked in only his loincloth, but he wanted to scream his triumph into that incandescent sky. Let Hades know that he had triumphed even over the task the gods had set him.

He threw his head back and opened his arms up, readied his scream...

And no.

Was this a mistake... a trick... had he beaten this thing or was his labor over?

After all these years he had learned to doubt his successes. What was success anyway? He'd always thought that for him to be successful someone else must fail. Now it felt more like success was something internal. He had done it—finally pushed the boulder to the top of the hill.

"It is a first step," came a melodious voice from behind him.

He whirled around and found Persephone picking her way up his trail behind him. She was a glowing presence, her beauty untouched by the years she had been bound here as wife of Hades. Her long blonde hair cascaded in soft curls around her shoulders. Her gaze was cornflower blue and filled with compassion and love, so much so that her single venture out of Hell each year renewed the earth and brought the springtime. She had high cheekbones that tilted her eyes and a full-lipped mouth that was curved in a beatific smile that made him want to smile back—do anything to keep her smiling.

"I told Hades that you had learned over the years, for what is there to do when one eternally pushes a boulder up a hill but to reflect on one's life and merits?" She tilted her head, her long blue robes shifting to silver and indigo as she lifted them to step closer. "I see by your eyes that you have learned—something, but not everything, I think."

She shook her head. "Such a stubborn, stubborn man and with so many traits to be undone. Yes, the land is eternal and much of what man does is futile, but there is still worthiness amongst men. Not all are as you were, friend Sisyphus."

She reached him and looked him up and down. "You've changed in other ways, as well, I see. The years, in some ways, have been good to you."

Sisyphus looked down at himself. His rough brown beard fell down to mid chest, his hair felt wild and matted with sweat about his head, but instead of an old man's body after all these centuries of labor, his muscles had grown hard, his body lean from physical effort.

He nodded but said nothing, for the gods and goddesses were fickle and quick to anger. Better to be silent and let her have her say.

Persephone stepped up beside him onto the rim of the hilltop and then circled him, studying. She shook her head. "How many more lifetimes will it take for you to find an ounce of kindness for your fellow man?"

He wasn't exactly sure what she meant. Man—men—and women, too, for that matter, were the source of too many problems when in reality they were too insignificant to ever really matter. He understood that now.

Persephone shook her head sadly. "Poor Sisyphus. I suppose it is time for another kind of labor."

She lifted her long-fingered hand and placed a cool palm upon his sweating forehead. "It is time, husband. You promised not to leave him on this hillside forever."

The sky rumbled. Lightning flashed and Sisyphus jerked back.

The bolt of lightning caught him in the chest. Pain seared through him. He smelled burned flesh.

The incandescent sky went black.

———

In the Underworld darkness, Persephone shook her head at the smoking space on the hilltop. At the end, even the dead were afraid of dying again. But itwas different with Sisyphus. She had watched the man labor for millennia. She had watched the arrogance burn out of him as his muscles seized, as the boulder crushed him and still he did not beg for succor, only gritted his teeth and labored on when many in this hellish landscape would have done anything, made any bargain, to escape their fate. His stoicism had led her to fondness for him, and, recently, to bargains with her husband. The god of the underworld loved his games of chance and so she had proposed a wager over Sisyphus.

Let the ancient, arrogant king return to life to see if he had learned the lessons Hades had set for him. Watching Sisyphus over the years gave her hope that he had learned to care and might even love. She prayed it was so, for Hades had laughed and lorded it over her when she suggested such a thing. He had pointed out that she could not even leave his country herself except for bringing the spring once each year. He called her a fool and no worthy judge of men. In her anger and haste to prove him wrong, she had done the unthinkable.

She had wagered with her own soul.

If Sisyphus could find it within him to love, then Persephone might have more time above with the living. If Sisyphus failed, then her time in the living regions would be cut in half. She dared not even think of what this would mean for those abiding above. Perhaps her foolish wager proved Hades point—she was a fool.

Across the black nether fields and ruby glow of the burning pits came the stench of burning flesh and the despairing wails of the dead. They seared through her as they always had until, after all these millennia, she felt madness was almost upon her. What would happen if she lost her mind? Would spring never come again? Hades cared little if more men and women died. Their deaths only increased his kingdom.

And if she lost her wager, what would happen to the world she loved? No spring, either?

She looked back at the boulder and vacant space beside the deeply rutted track.

"Sisyphus, my friend, your burdens have been many to build your strength. I pray you are strong enough to carry the world and our lives on your shoulders."

1

———————

Catherine "Cat" Moore nursed her first cup of coffee of the day as she stood on the main raised wood deck of her house. The sunrise was behind her, but the angled light turned the silken waters of Davis Bay golden. Far out across the waking dark blue water of Georgia Strait, the bulk of Vancouver Island lifted its white-capped mountains. The sunlight caught on the snowfields and on the windows and white sides of the buildings in island communities like Nanaimo, Parksville, and Comox. The air smelled of her coffee overlaid on the wind's briny scent of seaweed and the sweet of muffins baking from the coffee shop down the hill. It was going to be a good day, a typical Sunshine Coast day.

And it took everything she had to stand out here and face it.

Yes, she could enjoy the view from her living room's broad windows. That was how she did it most of the time. But once a day, rain or shine, she forced herself to stand out in the open like this. It was a test. Proof to herself that she could do it and not die.

But the vulnerability of it made her feel like running, keening, back into the house.

From the house next door came the sound of a sprinkler and the pleasant humming of Mrs. Whitcomb. Elizabeth Whitcomb was an avid gardener who seemed to live outside from early April to late October, planting and tending her flowers and vegetable patch. Cat had expressed an interest in learning more about gardening and Mrs. Whitcomb had offered to teach, but so far, she hadn't taken the older woman up on her offer.

An eagle's cry startled Cat and her heartbeat spiked. Her breath came in rough little gasps.There it was. The bald eagle perched in a tree along the water.It suddenly took flight, its white head and tail catching the sun. She tracked it across the sky, envying the bird its ability to escape to freedom. But to be so visible…

Her knuckles whitened on her favorite blue cup and she was stoopid, stoopid, stoopid for standing out here like a sitting duck. Anything could happen.

Purposely slowing her footsteps to a normal pace, she retreated into her house and stood just inside the glass door, breathing as if she'd run a race. It was like that every time, and every time she questioned why she did it to herself. Why force herself outside when it hurt so much?

But the answers were everywhere inside her house.

The living room filled the rear of the house just inside the sliding glass doors with the dining room to the left and the open kitchen in the corner. A long hall from the living room cut through the house past the bedrooms to the front of the house and the street. The great room of living room, dining room, and kitchen she had painted in pale turquoise like the Caribbean Sea when the water was shallow and the sun hit it just right. She'd been there often enough, traveling first with friends and then on her own down to Aruba, Curacao, and the Dominican Republic. The collection of shells in a series of square glass vases reflected it. But she'd been farther afield, too. A small, carved wood, Thai spirit house sat perched on the top of a bookcase. Tapestries brought back from Zimbabwe and India adorned the walls alongside her own artwork. A tall, blue, Chinese celadon vase had pride of place on the mantle above her fireplace. And underpinning it was a comfortable cream-colored couch and two navy tub chairs set on an ornate plush carpet she'd had shipped from Turkey.

Before, she had traveled extensively. Before, she had lived with a backpack eternally half-packed so that she could leave for somewhere at a moment's notice. Before,she was whole and sound of body and mind.

But that was before.

Clenching her eyes shut, she turned from the living room back to the view. At least the view made this house and her things seem less like a prison and more like a place she'd chosen to be. But then, it seemed like it was probably both, just layered on top of each other. She'd chosen this place three years ago as her refuge.

She hadn't expected it to become her prison, but increasingly that was what it was becoming.

Four years ago, after the events that had sent her into the hospital for two long weeks, fear had stopped her from returning to work as a probation officer. When she'd returned home to her Langley townhouse thirty minutes outside of the rich enclave of Vancouver, she'd found herself increasingly uneasy and downright afraid. As the fear grew and she withdrew from her social life, she'd realized that she was becoming reclusive to the point she had begun to wonder if she was agoraphobic. Thankfully, the government had provided her with a disability pension as a result of her injuries on the job and this allowed her to live. Following her counselor's advice and in hopes of regaining a normal life, she'd sold her house and come here, to the Sunshine Coast and this house.

Unfortunately, the move didn't seem to have worked.

Apparently, fear could find you no matter how lovely your surroundings.

A movement in her backyard brought her back to the window. Something was walking along the base of her rear fence, but it was half-screened by the curtain of blackberries she kept promising herself that she'd cut back. So far the bramble limbs had covered the garden patch of perennial flowers the previous owners had planted, though here and there she caught a glimpse of purple flowers poking their heads out through the glossy blackberry leaves.

Whatever was under the brambles reached her side fence and stopped. Or at least the movement stopped.

Then the brambles stirred a moment and a brindle-colored muzzle poked out of the brush followed by two golden eyes.

Coyote?

But the muzzle was too broad. She sipped her coffee absently and the creature in her yard eased out from the blackberries. Not a coyote—she had the wrong species entirely. Not canine, but feline. Still with kitten-spot camouflage, but no longer the cute kitten at all. Long tail, svelte body perfect for easing through trees. Large paws perfect for hunting, except one of the paws was held up beneath its belly. The young cougar limped into her yard and collapsed in the dappled shade of the old apple tree.With the shadows of its coat, it was almost invisible. It licked its injured paw and then stretched out on its side. Protruding rib bones rippled its tawny speckled hide.

Injured and weak.

It probably hadn't eaten in a while. Didn't that make them dangerous?

Probably, but still less dangerous than men were.

She hugged herself, fighting back her anxiety. Call conservation: that would be her best move. She retrieved her iPad from its docking station and searched for animal conservation. A government number came up, and she grabbed her phone and called.

After ten rings she got impatient. After fifteen, she hung up. What to do? Beneath the government Google listing was a second listing, this one for an animal conservation and rehabilitation center called *Wild Heart*. A name like that certainly wasn't government. She clicked on the listing and a website came up, complete with photos of owls and eagles, raccoons, and even a coyote. A slick-looking "about" page spoke of a mission to preserve Sunshine Coast environment and wildlife, and educate the public about their importance. The organization was privately owned and had been created by its owner nine years before.

She tried the government number again and this time got a recording that said the officers were out of the office and please leave a message. She did, but the cougar in her backyard wasn't looking so good. It lay there panting as if it was in seriously bad shape. If it had injured a paw like that, what else was wrong with it? She didn't want it to die.

She sighed and hung up, then went back to the website and pulled up the contact number for Wild Heart and punched in the number. The phone burred into her ear, once, twice. A click came at the end of the line.

"Wild Heart Conservancy," said a rumbly male voice.

It stopped her for a moment. Did she really want to deal with some stranger, a man who didn't even have the credentials of government? On the other hand, she couldn't leave the young cougar to die.

"Uh, hi. My name is Cat—Cat Moore. There's a young cougar in my backyard and it's clearly injured. It's just lying there and I'm afraid it might die. It looks very thin."

There was silence a moment. "You're sure it's a cougar and not a big house cat?" There was doubt in the voice as well as interest.

"Not too many house cats get to this size." She looked at the phone. Just who was this guy, doubting her? "He looks more like he'd eat a housecat for lunch—if he could catch it—but he's got a badly injured paw. Who knows what else has been injured." Silence reigned on the phone as if he was hesitating. "Before you ask, I tried government conservation, but no one was there."

"Sorry. I was just thinking about what I'll need and how to reconfigure the holding pens. Where are you?"

Cat swallowed and her hands shook on the phone. Giving her address to a strange man. Wasn't that how bad things happened?

But the cat's tawny side baked in the rising heat of the morning. She couldn't live with herself if she let the animal die. She knew what it was like to be left hurt and bleeding. She knew what it was like to be helpless and certain she was going to die.

"I'm in Davis Bay," she almost whispered. Then she swallowed and gave her address.

"I'll be right over," the voice said.

"I'll be watching for you."

The line went dead and she stared at the phone in her hand. Then her hand started to shake. Then not just her hand. What the heck had she just done?

She set her coffee cup down and went back to the window over the yard. The sky was impossibly blue. The sun was hot even through the southwest-facing glass. But goosebumps covered her arms as she hugged herself.

The fear sent her heart racing. Again.

2

———————

It was a great blue day when Sy Foster rumbled up to the Davis Bay address. Blue sky, blue ocean, and a garden with blue and gold blooms swaying across the street from the gray house with the blue door where supposedly a cougar was waiting for him.

The gray house looked like it had been painted in the past few years, but otherwise the property looked a little gone to seed. The grass was about four days too long. The garden, though planted with flowers, could use a good weeding. Though the curtains were open, it was odd that none of the windows were open on a day when, regardless of the ocean breeze, it was already hot. It was always good to let in the cooler morning breeze. He'd come to realize that breezes were good and cool ones even better. Even though this civilization had developed air conditioning to deal with the heat, natural cooling was far and away better.

Fit for a king, some would say.

He snorted at his feeble joke and turned off the engine of the battered white Ford truck. The sound of the ocean rose up the hillside from the bay. Seagulls cried. So did an eagle. He closed his eyes and inhaled the sea air and questioned, again, how he could have missed out on the simple pleasures millennia ago. All he could come up with was that he was so self-involved and busy being kingly that he simply hadn't noticed. How many mornings like this had he missed?

Most likely a lot.

He climbed out and thunked the door shut behind him. A curtain twitched in the front window, but he couldn't see anyone. The voice on the phone had been cool and deep for a woman. Nice. Sexy, even, though the voice probably went with some eighty-year-old recluse. There were a lot of seniors here on the Sunshine Coast. The place was overrun with them. A regular gray tsunami.

Course, they had nothing on him for age.

He walked up the walk and knocked on the door. A small sticker by the door announced the home was alarmed and monitored. Surprisingly, the door didn't immediately open. Instead he waited. And waited.

Impatiently, he knocked again.

"Who is it?" came a female voice through the door.

Well, damn it all to hell, who did she think it was?

"Sy Foster of Wild Heart Conservancy. You called me about a cougar." The urge to roll his eyes was almost overwhelming. Instead he rolled his neck and shoulders.

The lock clicked and the door pulled open a few inches.

"Do you have identification?" asked the cool voice from the phone. By the glimpse of a single doe-brown eye and a long length of untanned leg, this definitely wasn't one of the wave of seniors inundating the Sunshine Coast. Nope. This was definitely something else.

He fished in his pocket for his driver's license and held it out to her. Slim fingers snagged the identification from him and it disappeared inside for a moment. Then the door opened farther. A pair of large brown eyes looked up at him with the unusual combination of fear and determination. A jagged one-inch scar cut through her left brow and up into the smooth expanse of her forehead.

"You look younger than your photo," she said.

"Good genes, I guess." He shrugged.

She handed him back his driver's license.

"I'm Catherine Moore. People call me Cat." She held out that slim-fingered hand as if she was daring herself. The other hand fluttered up toward her head until she seemed to force it to her side.

When he caught her offered hand, her fingers were cool and he was almost certain he felt her shiver, but she pulled away so quickly he wasn't sure.

"So this cougar…" he said.

"Is still flaked out in my backyard."

He nodded, waiting for the invitation inside. Cat Moore sidled and wouldn't meet his gaze. "You can go around the side of the house to the backyard."

He shook his head. "I'd like to see what I'm dealing with, if that's okay by you." He tilted his forehead at the door.

Dismay spread across her features. She was a pretty blonde woman, about five-foot-eight, square jawed and with a delicate aquiline nose that had a small crook in it that suggested it had once been broken. On some women it might be a defect, but on her it was a charming flaw in an otherwise almost perfect oval face. She wore a pair of swirl-patterned, pink athletic shorts with a simple, white, short sleeved smock top that came down to her hips. When she moved, the top shifted to reveal slim curves and her legs were carved with muscle. Clearly an athlete, but there was a softening of her limbs as if, like the house, she was also going fallow.

Her throat worked a moment and then she swallowed and nodded. "All right."

She stepped aside to allow him to enter, but stepping past her he heard rapid breathing. A scent of roses marred by metallic fear came off her skin.

She stepped briskly past him and quickly led him from the front door to the rear of the house. The house had apparently been remodeled so that the living room, dining room, and kitchen were open concept and enjoyed expansive views of the ocean.

"Nice layout. Nice view," he said.

She nodded. "It's why I bought the house." But her expression said it wasn't the complete truth and he wondered why she'd lie about something as simple as that.

The living room and kitchen had sliding glass doors. She opened them but didn't step out. "The cougar's under the apple tree."

He stepped out and the door slid shut behind him, separating him from the woman. Weirder and weirder. He glanced back but crossed to the railing. The view was very nice indeed, with the competing bands of blue ocean, distant blue of Vancouver Island, blue-stained clouds, and the sky above. Lovely.

She hadn't lied. In the shade of the apple tree, a young cougar sprawled. The spotting that all cougar cubs had at birth was still evident on the coat, though they were fading. That put the cat at probably five to seven months old. Of course the faded spots could hold on for about two years, but by the size of this cat, he or she wasn't full grown.

"So what happened to you?" he asked. The cougar didn't move. Not even a tail twitch. A wild animal like this would usually be up and seeking escape at the proximity of a human.

"Hey!" he shouted. Still nothing. Clearly something was wrong with this one.

Shaking his head, he turned back to the house. Through the glass, the sunlight caught Cat Moore so her pale skin seemed to glow. She hesitated the barest fraction of a moment before opening the door for him. Clearly, she did not like people in her house.

"He's still there, isn't he?"

Sy nodded, contemplating how to approach this.

"You'll help him?"

He looked back at her and smiled. "We'll certainly try. Trouble is, I'd usually tranq him for safety and then load him up, but at the moment I'm not sure he can handle the drug if he's as weak as he looks.

"The alternative is I try to net him first and see what happens. If he doesn't fight, we still might get him in a cage; but it could be a near thing." He shook his head, kicking himself as an idiot for not believing her when she'd told him it was a cougar. "I should have brought a crew to help me."

"I—I can help. I'm reasonably strong."

He nodded. "Okay. We'll try the net. If we get close, I'll administer a low dose of tranq to keep him out."

Without waiting for her, he headed for the front of the house and left the door open expecting her to follow him. Instead, when he got to the truck, she wasn't with him. She stood inside her doorway looking as if she was fighting to remain there. Then she took a deep breath and stepped outside onto the doorstep.

"Give a hand would you? There's a bunch of stuff we'll need."

She hesitated and then stepped out of the shadow of the house into the sunshine and hurried down the walk to his truck, scanning the streets as she went as if expecting something unpleasant.

Her pulse raced in her neck when she reached him and it didn't slow down. Her pupils were huge as a cat sensing danger.

"You okay?" he asked as he hauled the soft net out of the truck. It was made of tough nylon and steel mesh and resistant to the sharpest claws and teeth.

"Fine."

She'd tried for emphatic, but it came out with a quaver. This woman was anything but fine. As fine as the seriously injured cougar in her yard?

Well, he was here for the cougar, not the woman.

"Carry this, please." He handed her his metal kit of needles.

"Are… are you a vet?" she asked.

He shook his head and headed for the path that led around the side of the house and presumably to the backyard.

"How—how do you know you're doing the right thing, then?" she asked as she trailed behind him, looking over her shoulder.

What was wrong with this woman? She looked fit and had the direct gaze of someone confident. In the house she'd actually seemed confident, but now…

He stopped at a yellow painted board gate that blocked his view of the yard and looked down at her. "Years of experience working with animals." Those brown eyes of hers with their huge pupils were pools he could drown in. She was lovely, but he had no time for women. He was on this earth to focus on the land and its other denizens, not people. He inhaled her soft scent of baby powder and green apple and sighed. "Listen, I get the feeling that this is hard for you. If you'd rather go back inside and wait until I'm finished, that's okay by me."

She blinked and, surprisingly, visibly straightened. Her shoulders squared. "No. No, I called you and the poor animal is on my property. If he needs help, I should be there to help you."

He frowned down at her. For all her uncertainty, he certainly hadn't expected her to follow through with this.

"Okay." He turned back to the gate and the latch, but the darn gate didn't open.

"Here. Let me show you." She stepped up beside him and reached through the small space at the edge of the gate with one hand while the other hand reached for the latch. Her hand landed on his and she went stone-still.

Warm hand, far warmer than he'd expected from a woman who looked like she was half-frozen—with fear? He was suddenly more aware of her nearness, of the rose scent of her long fall of hair and of the smoothness of the skin at the neck of her tunic. Her wide gaze snapped to his and the flutter of her pulse was too fast to count.

He eased his hand from under hers and eased back a pace. He'd seen looks like that on newly captured animals—distrust and fear. What could have this lovely woman so afraid?

She tore her gaze from him and back to the gate, did something to the latch, and the gate swung open in front of them to expose the breadth of the sunlit, uncut lawn.

He nodded. "Okay. First piece of business. You have to agree to do everything I say immediately when I say it. If I tell you to move, you move. If I tell you to freeze, you freeze. Understand?"

Her throat worked, but she nodded.

"Stay here by the gate until I tell you."

He grabbed the gate and rattled it on its hinges to get a response from the cougar, but the animal didn't move. "Leave the gate open. We might need to leave in a hurry depending on what happens."

He didn't wait for her nod, just set off, whistling, across the lawn. Some people talked. Some people sang. His tuneless whistle was to warn the cat he was coming. The yard was a broad space that fell gradually toward the rear fence where blackberry brambles fell over the wood boards from the neighbor's. The upper edge of the yard had the view of the ocean. It would be a nice place for a second deck down here by the walk-out basement. The apple tree grew about halfway down the yard and created a pool of shade in the otherwise brilliantly lit lawn. The young cougar lay sprawled in the grass.

Every few steps Sy stopped and waited to see if there was a response from the animal. None came. This cat was clearly in dire condition. He glanced over his shoulder. Like the woman?

Cat stood slender and unmoving at the corner of the house, tentative as a fawn in a clearing.

Not his concern. He focused back on the cat and kept on walking. The overlong grass brushed against his booted ankles. Here and there a bright dandelion bloomed golden in the dark grass. The blackberries at the rear of the yard needed a serious trimming. He reached the edge of the apple tree's shadow and paused, his whistle sounding overloud in his ears. Still, the cougar didn't move.

Taking the net off his shoulder, he swung a loop over his arm and swung it back and forth to build up momentum. On the next swing toward the cougar he released the netting and it swung out in a neat, circular sweep that fell squarely over the cat.

The cougar's head came up. It shook itself. It pawed once at the netting and then groaned loud and long before its head went down and it rolled onto its side. A far too-pale pink tongue lolled from the cat's mouth and its side rose slowly and slumped with each breath. A low rumbling purr came from the animal, an attempt to heal and comfort itself and apparently all it had the energy to do.

"Hey boy," he said, choosing a gender for the animal when he wasn't really sure. "You're not doing so good, are you?"

The cat's round, black ears flickered toward him and then went still.

Sy glanced over his shoulder again and motioned Cat to approach. She moved silently across the lawn and handed him his medical case.

He set the metal tool case down and snapped it open as he kept an eye on the cougar. The animal had to be very far gone to not rouse and try to fight the net, let alone escape the presence of humans, but he wasn't taking any chances.

He hauled out the syringe he'd prepared at his office, closed the kit, and slowly approached the animal. At its hip, he slowly stooped and slid the injection in the cougar's thigh.

The cougar leapt up to sitting, jerking the syringe out of his hands. Sy scrambled back, putting himself between the animal and Cat, who seemed frozen in place. The animal tried to stand, fighting the net. It lunged forward but its front legs caught in the netting. It staggered, then fell back on its haunches where it shook its head and then slowly, in stages, toppled sideways as the drug took effect. Its bony ribs rose and fell slowly.

He had to pray he hadn't given the animal too much tranquilizer, but he waited to the count of twenty before approaching again. He snagged the syringe out of the animal's leg, but this time the cougar didn't move.

"Time to move him. We've got maybe twenty minutes."

He motioned Cat back to the corner of the house in case the cougar woke and jogged back to his truck for a dolly and cage he'd rigged much like an ambulance stretcher. Then he hauled it back down the path along the side of the house before wrangling it through the thick grass to the cougar's side.

He checked the cat's eyes and pulse. Still out. He motioned Cat back over. "I'll need your help to get the cat into the cage. Are you okay with that?"

She looked at him and for the first time a small, charming smile crept into the corner of her mouth. "What would you do if I said no?"

He looked down at the animal. "Work a little harder and faster myself, but together we can get him safely in the cage much faster."

She nodded. "So what do you need me to do?"

"I'm going to strip the net off. Once that's done I want you to grab his hind end and I'll grab the front. We're going to lift him into the cage. Okay?"

She nodded, and wonder of wonders, helped him untangle the net from the cougar,then waited, ready, as he opened the cage door. At his nod, she grabbed the cat's hind legs, braced her legs, and lifted just as he hefted the front end. The cougar was lighter than he'd expected. Clearly the animal hadn't been eating regularly. They slid the animal across the grass to the cage and the two of them wrestled the animal inside. Then he leaned in to examine the cougar's leg. Deep gashes had cut almost to the bone and infection had set in.

Not good; and just as bad were the gashes in its side that the animal had clearly tried to tend by licking. Unfortunately, it looked like abscesses had formed under the newly healed skin. Clearly there were a lot of problems here that were going to require extensive—and costly—veterinarian care. Not exactly what he needed when his overhead costs were constantly mounting. He straightened from his cursory exam and slid the cage door shut. He fastened the clip that locked it closed and looked back at Cat.

"She's in bad shape."

She nodded, her gaze never leaving the cougar. "What will you do?"

"Get her back to my place and call the vet. Then we'll see if it's possible to save her. It's a female."

She looked up at him. "You mean she might not live?"

He shook his head. "The reality is she might be too far gone in the vet's assessment. If that's the case, we'll have to euthanize. It's best for the animal. If the vet says there's a chance, then we'll get her settled and do what needs to be done."

"No." She shook her head.

She was so emphatic that he could almost imagine her as a child stomping her foot.

"No. This animal has to live."

There was almost a little panic around the edges of this woman.

"Death is part of the natural order of things," he said gently. "The best we can do is make good use of the time we are given." Like a millennium or two to even understand what you were doing wrong. He sighed.

"Listen, we'll do the best we can. That's all we can do."

Her gaze went suddenly distant and glassy. She stilled, except for a hand that trailed up to her face. Then her gaze locked on his and she smiled sadly.

"You're right, of course. I guess that's all anyone can do, isn't it?"

But it was as if he'd disappointed her and suddenly he didn't want to do that. "Listen, help me get the cougar up to my truck. I'll give you my phone number and you can call to get updates." He didn't offer to call her because there was something about Cat Moore that said she wouldn't give out her telephone number to a man she just met.

Cautious. That was how he'd describe her if anyone asked. Cautious and sad and—and a little trapped? He wondered what her past was and what mistakes she had made because, like him, she was clearly pushing her own stone up a hill.

———

Sy stood too close beside her as they hauled on the ropes attached to the jury-rigged dolly and cage contraption. His scent of old-fashioned spicy aftershave and the cougar musk filled her nose and she found herself too aware of him. It had been a long time since she'd been this close to any man. Even as she strained against the ropes and the dolly that seemed determined to remain caught in the grass, a part of her was panicking at his nearness. But she held it together and hoped she proved herself more than a scatty female by her physical effort. Actually, it felt kind of good to be able to do something more than work out in her basement gym. Put the muscles she'd developed to good use.

The darn lawn was making sure of it.

"Sorry about the grass," she said after the dolly and cage had been snagged on a clump of grass for about the fifteenth time. "I really should get out to mow it, but sometimes… It's just…" She shook her head because it was hard to admit even to herself that irrational fear kept her from doing it.It was her own backyard for God's sake! "I don't get to it, I guess. Guess I better mend my ways or I'll have a jungle out here. I hadn't realized how bad it was. From the deck it just looks green and lush," she ended lamely and felt his regard like a hot brand on her face.

They were both sweating by the time they finally tore through the last of the grass impeding the dolly's wheels and the cage rolled easily on the gravel path along the side of the house and then up the paved driveway to Sy's truck.

A shiny, new, compact, blue Nissan pulled in, in front of his truck, and released a long, lean, frizzy-haired brunette with high cheekbones that any woman would envy.

"Jude!" Cat said. Jude Hebert had long been Cat's good friend and coworker at the Langley Probation Services before everything happened and Cat left her job. Since Cat's move to the Coast, they unfortunately hadn't seen as much of each other because Jude still called Langley home and a visit required a forty-minute ferry ride.

"Cat? Is everything all right?" Jude left her car, door still open, and rushed over to Cat. A big hug and then she turned a suspicious brown eye on Sy. "What's going on?"

Then she took in the cage and stopped. "Is that a…"

"It's a cougar, Jude. It's injured and it was in my yard. I called Sy, here, to come and get it."

"Jude Herbert," Jude said and stuck out her long, slim hand to Sy.

Sy accepted it cautiously and shook.

Jude eyed Sy and turned, brow-raised, back to Cat. Clearly Jude was assessing the man, just as Cat had done before she'd opened her door. Cat glanced back at Sy. He *was* tall and he significantly outweighed her. He was also fit and toned in that nice way that men get through constant hard work rather than scheduled exercise. But his gaze was largely open and reasonably kind—anyone who ran an animal refuge had to be—even though there was something about him that spoke of old pain—and secrets.

That made her hesitate. She'd seen a similar reserve in too many criminals over the years. There was something more about him, too. A magnetism that, with his thick dark hair that covered his ears and his chocolate gaze, likely had women flocking to him. She'd had criminal clients like that, too. They were the ones who took advantage of their female companions and invariably hurt them even if it wasn't always physical. But unlike with those manipulative clients, she could almost feel the pull toward Sy herself—if she could ever trust any man.

"So you're taking the cougar away now?" Jude asked stepping slightly in front of Cat and interrupting her thoughts.

"Back to the conservancy refuge, yes," Sy said. He leaned around Jude to Cat, his shaggy hair swinging boyishly into his eyes before he shoved it back. "If you're concerned, you can come and visit. Once the cougar is healthy enough, she'll be in one of the large cages where she can exercise. There are a bunch of other animals, too. A few young deer. An orphan bobcat kitten—orphaned by a well-meaning idiot who found the kitten alone probably right where the mother told it to stay, but he collected it. Damn fool." He shook his head. "Sorry. I just get frustrated at how people have lost all common sense when it comes to wildlife. They either think they should shoot it, or they want to raise it as a pet." He stopped himself. "But that's another story."

He used his dolly contraption and Cat and Jude stood back as it smoothly lifted the cage to truck bed level and slid the cage into the bed, the dolly legs folding neatly under it as he had clearly planned. He leaned into the truck to attach stabilization hooks, his lean rear end nicely filling out his khaki trousers.

"Nice bit of machinery," Cat said, meaning the dolly.

Jude choked and coughed beside her as Sy straightened. "It does the job."

"I'll bet it does," Jude muttered.

Cat threw her a scolding glance, then turned back to Sy. "Thank you for coming and getting the cougar. If you'll give me your number, I'll call to check up on her."

He retrieved a card from his truck cab and gave it to her. "We'll do everything we can. I'll make sure of it," he said and hesitated. "Thanks so much for calling. I'm glad I got here when I did. An animal injured like this—it needs care, you know?" Then he shook his head. "And I should go. The cougar needs attention and you've got company. It was nice meeting you, Cat Moore."

His gaze held hers a moment longer than necessary. Then he blinked and turned away. "Take care of yourself."

He climbed into the truck and it started with a rumble. The driver's side window rolled down and he waved as he drove off down the road.

The funny thing was, she was almost sad to see him and the cougar leave.

3

—————

"Earth calling Cat. Earth to Cat, come in?"

The voice brought Cat back from listening to the grumble of the truck's engine down the hill as it turned onto the highway. Did it turn left or right?

She didn't know and suddenly panic flooded in. She didn't know where the cougar was going! She'd sent the poor creature off with a stranger who could hurt it. Oh God, what had she done? What had she done?

The sun was too bright. The open sky too exposing. All the windows of the houses on the street hid people who could be spying and plotting.

Her breath caught in her throat and she couldn't fill her lungs. She coughed. Gasped for air and then suddenly Jude, blessed Jude, was there. "Come on. Let's get you inside. It looks like you've had enough excitement for one day."

Jude ran over to her car, grabbed a bag, and returned to sling an arm over Cat's shoulders and turn her toward the house. Down the front walkway toward the blue door that had held her safe and sound for the past year. Up the front steps and Jude pushed open the door.

Cat stopped. Was it holding her safe or keeping her a prisoner? She wasn't sure. She looked over her shoulder and caught a glimpse of Mrs. Whitcomb in her shady straw hat and long flowing shirt and trousers now tending her front garden.

Then Jude's pressure on her shoulders ushered Cat inside once more and all the comfortable bits of her life settled into place. The door clicked shut behind them and relief flooded in. The band around her chest loosened and she could breathe. Then she felt like crying. Was it always going to be like this? Her home might be safe, but… she *was* a prisoner.

Sighing, she turned Sy's card in her hands. *Wild Heart Conservancy and Animal Refuge*, read the card. Sy Foster was written at the bottom and an address and phone number were both there.

She followed Jude's slim back down the hall to the great room that overlooked the ocean. She knew where the cougar had gone, at least. And from the dark green card with its golden lettering, it at least looked like he was an established business. Mind you, given anyone could get a business card on line for fifteen dollars, maybe it didn't mean a darn thing.

That was her, suspicious by nature.

Jude had dumped her bag in the hallway and gone into the kitchen. Used to Cat's sudden silences, she ran water into the kettle and set it on the stove to boil. Her hair was a dark halo around her head.

"Tea, right?" Jude asked. "Settles the nerves and all that."

"Thank you, but it should be me offering you tea. This is my home," Cat said.

"And I've just made myself at home. My usual bedroom?"

Cat nodded down the hall and Jude collected her bag and headed for the bedroom near the front of the house. Cat went into the kitchen and put tea bags into the silver-gray raku teapot she'd bought on line. The kettle boiled and she poured water into the teapot as Jude returned to stand with her hands on her hips in the center of the room.

"Looks exactly the same. Still that perfect view. I have to say I was pleased to see you outside. Have you made it down to the ocean?"

Instead of meeting Jude's gaze, Cat busied herself preparing two cups of milk tea with honey. Finally, she shook her head. "I know that was the one thing the psychologist said I should try to do this past month but I couldn't get myself to leave the house."

Jude rounded the kitchen island and enveloped Cat in a hug. "I'm sure you tried, but this is getting worse, Cat. You're becoming a recluse when you're young and beautiful and alive and have so much to give."

Cat snorted and pulled away for the kitchen. "Barely alive, you mean. And I'll carry this scar for life." She touched the scar above her eyebrow.

Jude rolled her head toward the ceiling. "Now who's acting all 'poor me'? The scar's barely noticeable. I thought you told me that you weren't going to do that." She took her cup and returned to the living room to plop down on the cream couch. She sipped her tea and glanced up at Cat, her brown gaze mischievous. "Maybe you need to get a dog. That would get you out."

Cat rolled her eyes. "Like I need that headache. And I could just put the dog in the yard. So there."

She grabbed her cup and came around the island to lean against it. She shook her head and looked at her tea. Set the cup down. "The trouble is, I'm losing interest. The view's great, but I can't touch it or be part of it. The yard—I can't seem to get pride of place enough to mow it. Or pull the weeds in the garden out front or wash the windows or—or anything."

Jude scanned the room. "You do pretty well at housekeeping and by the look of you, you're keeping fit. You're doing something."

Sighing, Cat shook her head. "Okay. Let me amend what I said. I can't seem to get myself to do anything if it involves going outside. I've even started using home delivery for groceries and that's a step backward. At least I was getting out to shop when I first moved here." She hung her head. It was a sorry state of affairs and she didn't like looking like she was feeling sorry for herself. She straightened and walked over to the glass wall, dared to open the folding glass doors and let the environment spill inside. The air smelled faintly of ocean. The breeze carried the hum of lawnmowers and laughter from her neighbors on the other side. They were a young couple with young children. "That's about the best I've been able to do."

"You were outside when I got here."

When Cat glanced back at her friend, Jude had pushed her wild hair behind her ears and was peering at Cat over the rim of her cup.

"I was, but that was an extraordinary circumstance. The cougar was injured. It needed my help."

"It did, or the sexy animal refuge worker?" Jude asked with an arch of her brow.

Cat shook her head and looked back at the view, suspecting where Jude was going. "Both, I guess. But if he was sexy, I didn't notice."

"Really? That nice tight ass in those khakis? If I hadn't thought you were interested I'd have thrown myself at him myself…" Jude leered up at her, then set her cup down. She leaned forward on the edge of the couch and shook her hair loose. "Hi, big boy. I see you've got a thing for fur and restraints…" she said huskily.

Cat threw her gaze heavenward. "Jeezus-God, preserve us!" Then she looked back at Jude. "That kind of performance is sure to get you exactly nowhere. No wonder you're single!"

Grinning, Jude stood up and crossed to Cat to sling a warm arm around Cat's shoulders again. "Single by choice. Just like

I'm here by choice. I can step outside and drive away any time I want. I can go to the beach or the store and pick out my own darn broccoli or meat. Or men, for that matter. I don't have to wait for someone else to do it for me." She shook her head and her curls tickled Cat's cheek. "Don't you think this has gone on too long? You can't let that bastard ruin your life."

Cat stiffened. She tried very hard never to even think of the bastard in question, let alone speak of him. As it was, there were too many nights when he was too vividly present, haunting her dreams with his fists and his boots.

"That bastard took my life from me. He took my job, my community, my kidney, and my eye from me. How much more of a life can he ruin?" She glared up at Jude.

"But you've got a new community—or the potential of one. You've still got a functioning kidney and you can still see. Mostly."

"I'm flipping blind in one eye, Jude. You try living your life that way! You try living your life afraid that your other kidney will crap out on you like they say it could. You try living your life wondering whether the bastard who took it all away is coming back to finish the job!"

"I'm sorry, Cat." Jude had her eyes closed, her head bowed under her wealth of hair, as if Cat's words struck her.

"No. You're not, because we have this discussion every damn time you come for a visit. I know you feel guilty that you went home before me and left me to close up the office, but you don't need to be. If you'd waited you might be like me, or worse. Dead. Kyle Redburn was out to get the person who was recommending time in jail for his latest offence. He wasn't going to let some other woman stop him."

She pulled away from Jude's warmth and retreated to the kitchen to pour her tea down the sink. "You know what? I appreciate that you think you have to come over here to help me get over myself, but don't. You don't need to feel guilty. I'm a big girl. I can take care of myself."

Jude was looking at her with her steady brown gaze, the same gaze she turned on probation clients who were messing up big time. But Cat wasn't messing up. She didn't need so-called friends who came to get all up in her face about how she was living. She was just fine as she was. She had her house. She had her view. She had her so-called life.

Except it wasn't much of one and everything Jude had said was mostly true. She looked ruefully at her empty tea cup and sighed. "I'm sorry. I know you're trying to help and I know that what happened to me could have happened to anyone in our job and that things have changed since it happened so all probation officers are more secure, but it doesn't negate the fact that Kyle Redburn has never been arrested for what he did to me."

"He disappeared," Jude said.

"And he might never come after me, but he doesn't have to," Cat said softly. Because he'd managed to kill a key part of her— the part that had been brave.

Jude crossed the room and pulled her into a hug. "We'll never let him win, Cat. Never." She held Cat away from her. "Now pour yourself another cup of tea and let's drink it and do something wild—like mow that lawn of yours!"

Cat burst out laughing, but she did as she was told, and raised her cup at Jude. The two friends curled on the couch where they could enjoy the view and drink their tea reminiscing about the old days before it all happened.

Before Cat's life changed.

———

The sun had risen almost to noon when Cat found the syringe in the grass. She and Jude were both hot and sweaty, Cat from shoving the lawnmower through too-thick, too long green grass and Jude from lugging the heavy canvas bag of cuttings over to Cat's compost corner. Of course, the compost corner was overwhelmed by blackberry brambles so they had to cut them back before they could even begin to cut the lawn. By the time they'd finished, they'd both been left slashed and bloodied by the thorns.

"A cougar's looking downright friendly right about now," Jude complained as she'd wiped blood off yet another tear in her lily-white limbs. But they'd freed up the compost bin and had plans to perhaps tackle the brambles along the back fence the next day. If they could ever finish the darn lawn.

Cat was shoving the mower in front of her in yet another six-inch parallel line because the mower was overwhelmed by a broader path. She came into the dappled shadow of the apple tree where the grass was a tangle from the cougar's capture when she caught a glimpse of something silver in the grass. She paused the mower's drive and dug in the grass, coming up with a silver syringe that must have been what Sy used on the cougar after it was netted. It must have fallen out of Sy's pocket when they moved the animal and neither of them had noticed as they wrestled the cougar into the cage and then the cage out of the yard.

It was heavy in her palm and heated by the sun. Clearly not a disposable piece of equipment. Sy Foster would miss it.

"Whatcha got there?" Jude asked, climbing the slope up from the compost across the ragged area that Cat had finished cutting. If she started cutting regularly, the grass would even out, but at the moment it looked patchy and uneven given chunks of sod had pulled loose when the mower had simply pulled out and not cut the grass. Jude stopped and swiped the sweat from her eyes.

"A serious looking piece of equipment, I'd say," Jude said, critically eyeing the syringe, sweat running out from under her matted hair.

"Something that needs to be returned," Cat said.

"Good. An excuse to call him," Jude said with a knowing grin.

"I don't like the guy! I'm not looking for a reason to call him."

"Uh huh." Jude pursed her lips. "Seems to me the lady doth protest too much. As I recall you stepped away from him like you were scalded when you realized it was me who had arrived."

"I did not!"

"Did too. That's how I saw it."

"Well you saw it wrong. I'll give him a call to let him know it's here and maybe put it in the mail to him."

"Yeah, right." Jude snorted. "You do that."

She released the almost full grass catcher from the mower and trudged back down the hill to the compost.

"I will," Cat called. "You just watch me. I don't need a man in my life to be happy."

Jude's mocking chortle rose up the hill.

In response Cat doubled down her efforts and pushed and shoved the unwieldy mower through the grass until everything was cut right up to the edge of the stone, ground-level patio beneath the upper wood deck. That just left the strip of grass along the side of the house and the miniscule lawn out front. She did both, with Jude hovering nearby nursing a tall icy glass of water. When Cat was done, she shoved the mower back into the garage and sat beside Jude in the afternoon shadows that had fallen across the top step of the front porch.

"Not too close. You're hot and you smell of lawn clippings," Jude said.

"And you don't?" Cat said, snagging Jude's glass and draining the contents. "Thanks." Ice cubes clinked in the glass as she handed it back. The air smelled of mown grass and the honeysuckle burgeoning in Mrs. Whitcomb's yard. "That was a good day's work." The effort felt good—now that they were done.

"It was. And it didn't kill you to be outside," Jude said.

Cat turned a bramble-torn calf left and right, admiring the angry welt. "Almost."

"It did not kill you." Jude' voice was emphatic. "And you might get some color in your lily white legs, too."

"No," Cat allowed. "It did not kill me. I guess you're good for me. Forcing me out of my comfort zone."

Jude nodded. "Hold that thought because we're going out tonight."

Alarm jangled through Cat's limbs and her chest tightened. She stood up to peer down at her friend. "Did it never occur to you that this might be enough for one day?"

Jude smiled mildly. "I'm only here for a week, remember? The Langley Probation Office needs me, so I aim to work fast."

"Yeah. Right. I'm going to go take a shower." Shaking her head, Cat abandoned her friend and retreated into the house.

In the white tiled master bathroom with the soaker tub and glassed-in shower, Cat stripped off her clothes and examined the resentment she was feeling. Sometimes Jude was too much. She just didn't know when to quit. Wasn't it enough that Cat had spent the entire day outside in her yard, first with the cougar and then with the lawn?

She showered quickly, luxuriating in the rain shower, and then toweled off and padded into her bedroom with the king-sized bed draped in a white duvet over blue bedding. From the guest room came sounds that said Jude had followed her into the house. Water ran so Jude was having a shower, too. Feeling peevish, Cat went into her bathroom and grinned as she flushed the toilet and heard an answering yelp. Okay, a little revenge was always good.

Twenty minutes later she came out of her room dressed in navy leggings and a white t-shirt tied at the waist as she toweled her hair dry. Jude was out on the deck picking knots out of her hair and letting the breeze fluff her curls. She looked cool and carefree in a pair of white shorts and a red-and-white striped sleeveless top that had small blue fish on the straps. She sat in one of Cat's chairs with her long legs propped up on the porch railing.

Cat hesitated at the deck door, then caught herself and firmly stepped out. What was wrong with her? This porch was part of her house for goodness sake!

"You look ready for the beach," she said.

Jude glanced back at her, assessing Cat's attire. "You look good, but those leggings are going to get wet if we go to the beach."

"Maybe that's because I never agreed to go to the beach." Cat stepped up to the rail and studied her yard. Even with the grass mown she could see the tracks the rescue cage had taken across the lawn. There was where the cougar had lain and there was where Sy had stood with the sunlight and the apple tree shadows dappling his hair as he tossed the net so ably and then as he bent to inject the animal. He had been so cool under pressure. He hadn't even gotten scared when the cougar leapt up. In fact, she liked his calm demeanor—as if he'd seen a lot and nothing fazed him anymore. Working with animals, maybe he had. It was odd, but she'd actually felt steadier around him.

She turned back to Jude. "I'm really not sure about this beach idea. A day like this, everyone will be there."

Jude tipped a brow at her. "That's the point, isn't it? We'll be there just like everyone. One of the crowd." She hauled her legs down off the rail and stood. "It'll be fine, Cat. Just like old times."

Cat shook her head. In old times she hadn't had a permanent dent in her skull and she'd seen things bifocal. She'd been able to see things from both sides and that objectivity had been her reputation and her bread and butter as an officer of the court. Now her vision had narrowed down to the victim's perspective.

Jude put her arms around Cat and drew her into a hug.

"You're not a victim anymore. You're whole and alive. Don't waste your life."

She shoved back from Jude. "I'll think about it. First I have to phone cougar-guy and tell him I have his syringe."

Determined to get away from Jude's incessant coaxing and cajoling, Cat retreated to the house and the phone. She retrieved the business card from the kitchen counter and picked up her cell before heading to her favorite living room chair. It was a brocade easy chair of a turquoise-green the pale color of Caribbean wave foam. She had it facing the fireplace with a wicker footstool so that in winter she could put her feet up and read before the fire, with the ocean spread just beyond her sliding patio doors. With the chair reclined, she could imagine she was free again, floating on the ocean on a sunny day.

Today she perched tensely on the edge of the chair before punching the phone number from the card into her phone. The line drilled into her ear once, twice, three times and then there came the click of an answering machine.

"You have reached Wild Heart Conservancy and Animal Refuge. We're sorry we can't come to the phone right now. We're most likely busy with the animals. Please leave a message at the beep. For Jana, dial 211."

Cat eyed the phone. Jana? Who was Jana? But the line clicked for a message.

"Uh, Sy. This is Cat Moore. I, uh, I hope the cougar is okay. Thank you again for coming and rescuing her. I don't know what I would have done if she'd died here..." Horrible thought. She closed her eyes. "Listen. After today's struggle, I figured I better mow the lawn. So I did, but I found your metal syringe in the grass. I've got it here if you want it back. Please call me and let me know how I should return it to you." She left her number and hung up feeling breathless and tight in the chest.

When she looked up, Jude was standing in the doorway, her

long pale arms crossed over her chest, her wild brown curls catching the sun like a corona around her head.

"So. You've made your call. No more excuses. Grab your purse and let's head out."

With Jude, arguing was futile. Many a probation client had discovered that the hard way. So had her friends. When Jude had that expression on her face, there was no denying her.

Dragging her feet, Cat retrieved her purse. Jude ushered her out the front door and Cat swallowed as Jude took Cat's keys and locked the door.

"We'll take my car," Jude announced and led the way up the walk.

Heart thumping too hard in her chest, Cat followed. It felt like lead weighted her feet. Her palms were damp and she really needed to pee, but she made it to Jude's car and climbed inside before slamming the door closed.

Her breath came in short jagged gasps as Jude slid behind the wheel. Her stomach flip-flopped as the car started and Jude pulled away from the curb. She grabbed the door handle and hung on for dear life even though Jude was a careful driver and they were only going thirty miles an hour down the hill toward the water.

It took less than two minutes before Jude turned onto the two-lane road that was the highway, seeking a parking spot along the waterfront promenade. She pulled into an angle parking spot and turned the engine off. The car ticked around them, but through the windows came the sound of the waves and cries and laughter of children and their families playing on the sandbars exposed as the waves receded with the tide. Along the promenade was a steady parade of people, their strollers, and their dogs.

"I don't think I can do this, Jude." It was hard to speak, her voice almost a gasp.

"You do it the first time, then it won't be so bad," Jude said gently. "Come on. I'll be with you the entire time." She shoved open the driver's side door and climbed out, allowing in a cacophony of sound.

When Jude closed the door, Cat was tempted to lock her door, but that was futile, too, given Jude had the door clicker and keys. She pushed her door open and Jude caught it and swung it wide. The breeze on Cat's skin made her feel exposed. The sun felt like a spotlight. She should never have worn this white t-shirt because it just clamored for attention. People were looking at her and she needed to keep track of them to make sure she was safe.

There were the two women with the small gold-colored dog. There was the man striding out by himself with his camera. There was a young man slouched and not looking at anyone else as he strolled down the promenade. She didn't like the way his gaze skimmed right over her as if he was purposely pretending not to notice her.

No.

She didn't know this man and he wasn't Kyle Redburn. He was nothing to worry about.

But Kyle wasn't the only evil person in the world. There could be someone else. Someone who would finish the job and kill her.

But she let Jude catch her hand and urge her out of the car. By the time she stood, she was shaking and gasping for breath. Jude caught her shoulders.

"Look at me, Cat. Just look at me."

Cat managed to bring her wildly swinging gaze back to her friend. Jude smiled down at her, but Cat still could barely breathe because at the edge of her vision crowded all these strangers.

"Just look at me, Cat. Now copy my breathing. Big, big inhale. As big as you can."

Cat tried and choked and began to cough.

Jude held on and tipped Cat's head up so she could still look in Jude's eyes. "Exhale, Cat. Push it all out as much as you can."

Cat did and spluttered around the coughing. Caught her breath as Jude urged her to inhale again. Gradually her gasps steadied into regular breathing that was maybe a little too rapid, but she was getting oxygen. She nodded at Jude.

"Thanks. I should have you around for all panic attacks. Now are we done? Can we go home?"

Jude looked at her critically, then shook her head. "I think we're here now, so we'll try for a little stroll. Okay?"

No. No. NO! Cat wanted to say. Instead sheclosed her eyes when Jude caught her hand and led away from the safety of the car and onto the promenade, then down concrete stairs to the gravel and rock shoreline.

Cat opened her eyes. The wind was in her face, and if she looked out at the water, she didn't have to see all the people behind her. The skin prickled on the back of her neck, because people could see her. Heck, they *were* looking at her. Jude, meanwhile, was turning up stones to expose small crabs and snails. Seagulls and crows squawked overhead and fell on the booty Jude's efforts revealed.

There was driftwood, too, scattered across the rocks, and Cat took a tentative step toward an interesting looking piece. A huge black dog went bounding past her and almost bowled her over.

"Cody! Cody, come on!" Masculine voice. A male shadow spread across the shore toward her and her heart started pounding. Rocks scraped behind her and suddenly a man was beside her.

"Sorry about that," he said with a grin. "He's young."

So was the guy. About Kyle's age and Kyle's height. Similar dark hair and build.

Cat's hand reached her mouth about the time the scream strangled in her throat. Then Jude was there pushing her way between Cat and the young man. She said something Cat couldn't hear over the roaring in her ears, and then Jude had an arm around Cat's shoulders and was leading her back to the car.

Inside, the roar of ocean and voices cut out a little and Cat drew in a ragged breath. "Y-you see what I mean? T-too many people."

"A normal amount of people." Jude shook her head, her hair like corkscrew coils around her shoulders. "You just need to get used to them again. You've locked yourself in for too long."

Locked herself in or locked the world out? There was a distinction and Cat was pretty sure she'd done the latter.

"Shall we get some groceries? I'll let you pick out the produce."

The thought of checkout crowds was exhausting, but Jude started the car and drove the short distance to Cat's grocery store and parked.

"Maybe you should do the shopping this time," Cat said.

Jude must have seen something in Cat's face, for she nodded and squeezed Cat's wrist. "I won't be long. I'm thinking steak for dinner. You've got red wine at home, right?"

Cat wasn't sure, but Jude waved away her protests. "It's okay. I brought a few bottles over with me. They're in the back."

Then she was out the door and striding oh-so-confidently across the parking lot to the store's sliding glass doors.

Cat leaned back and closed her eyes. There was no way that she'd ever be that confident again. Kyle had stripped that away from her just as certainly as he'd stolen her official identification after he'd beaten her almost to death.

She opened her eyes and across the lot under the awning of the supermarket stood Kyle.

She bolted upright. It was him, surely as if was her sitting here in Jude's car. Same breadth of shoulder. Same height. Same mesmerizing gaze that had lured a dozen women into isolated corners where they were sexually assaulted. She quickly scrunched down in hopes he wouldn't see her, but he already had. *He was looking right at her!*

She flushed with the memory of how he'd stripped down her

broken body and touched her—just to prove that he had all the power and she had nothing.

The brilliant afternoon went black and night had fallen and she was abandoned in the office back parking lot unable to move. Unable to save herself. Left as Kyle had left her. Her ears still ringing with his laughter. She hadn't known whether she would die there alone. Had thought she was dead until the jangle of a shopping cart brought her to consciousness again.

"Help me," she'd whispered and, praise God, the homeless woman with the cart had called 911.

The driver door pulled open and Cat yelped and huddled against her door. *Get her feet up and kick him before he could get her.*

Jude plopped into the car. She handed in a couple of plastic shopping bags.

"What a madhouse in there," Jude said. Then she caught Cat's expression.

"Cat? Cat, what happened?"

"He's here." Cat could barely force the hoarse words out.

"He? He who?" Jude glanced through the window at the shoppers

Cat couldn't bring herself to look back at the supermarket. She lifted her chin. "Under the awning. Tell me that isn't Kyle."

Cat held her breath as Jude casually shifted her gaze toward the store. Her gaze held. Then she frowned and turned back to Cat. "Who are you talking about? I don't see Kyle."

Cat shifted around to look and but the only man standing there was with his girlfriend and they were both blond.

"He must have left. He was probably afraid that I'd call the police. Which I'm going to do right now!" She hauled out her phone. But Jude caught her hand.

"Hold on a moment. Are you absolutely positive it was Kyle Redburn? He hasn't been seen in this province for over two years. Ever since that night. What would bring him back now?

Here?" Jude shook her head and held up her hand to stop Cat from stating the obvious. Kyle Redburn had come back to finish what he started two years ago. And if he hadn't known before, she'd just confirmed that she was here by coming to this stoopid store.

"Before you go to your dark place, think about it, Cat. How would he ever know to come here? You moved and didn't leave a forwarding address. All your mail came to me and I packed it up and sent it to you."

"I still bought my house under my name." She stabbed her finger at Jude."I opened a bank account here and have my victim's pension and disability come here. He could have connections in the post office or elsewhere. Or someone could have let the information slip that I'm here. It's not that hard to find a person if you try. We did it for years with our jobs. You still do."

Jude grabbed Cat's hands and held on.

"Okay. Okay. If it's Kyle, what do we do?"

Cat held up her phone. "Number one, call the police. Number two, get the heck back to my house where it's safe. Better still, you drive while I make the call."

Bless Jude. She drove.

4

───────────

S y knocked on the house's blue door once more, then turned
to scan the neighborhood. Nice places, all of them with the
well-cared for look of owners who had the wealth of too much
time and not enough planned to fill the days. Newly retired, most
of them, he'd bet. Come to the Sunshine Coast for the ocean
view that they couldn't afford in Greater Vancouver. Clumps of
lilies swayed in the breeze. Tall, drought resistant grasses were
tufted in silver. Green lawns glistened. Somewhere down the
street a lawnmower hummed. A crow cawed overhead and
settled on a power line, its black body silhouetted against the
blue, cloudless sky.

And still no sound from inside the house. There was no sign
that Cat Moore even had a car, unless it was locked up tight in
the garage. However, there was no sign of the spiffy little blue
car Cat's friend, Jude, had arrived in, so perhaps they had
gone out.

He'd been an idiot to come. A special trip into town simply
because of a voice on his answering machine. For a syringe that,
yes, he wanted back, but he had six others like it back at the

refuge. He didn't *need* it. But he'd kinda liked that Cat Moore had called.

And so he'd made a fool of himself and come. Jana would laugh out loud if she knew what he'd done. She'd been after him for what felt like eons to get out and meet someone and he'd assured her time and again that he wasn't so inclined.

Apparently, he'd misrepresented himself because here he was, seeking another glimpse of those huge brown eyes and that half-glimpsed smile. He wanted to understand why she looked so, well, worried. He was pretty certain it was something more than the cougar.

"She's not here. She and that friend of hers went out."

He craned to see where the voice came from and a woman stood up from beyond a screen of flowers in the next yard. She wore long sleeves and a broad-brimmed straw hat that shadowed her features. She eased her back and nodded. From what he could see, she fit the age demographic for the neighborhood. Cat was an anomaly there, too.

"They left about an hour ago."

An hour. Approximately right about the time Cat had left the message. Of course, she had the refuge address. What if she'd left to bring him the syringe while he had come here?

He closed his eyes and set aside the flutter of excitement in his chest. It was something he hadn't felt since before a certain boulder had to be rolled up a certain hill. Back then, the excitement arose whenever there was something he wanted and possibly couldn't have. It had been the challenge that excited him.

Was this the same? If so, it was to be avoided. Winning what he wanted was what had landed him in Hades and here to repent for that life.

He thanked the woman, rapped the door a final farewell, and headed for his truck. This had been a mistake that he wouldn't make again. The fact that Cat wasn't here was almost a blessing.

He was just climbing into the cab when a low-slung blue Nissan cruised up the hill and pulled in behind him. He recognized the car and its occupants.

"Sy? What're you doing here?" The owner of the house climbed out of the passenger side door. Although her clothes looked cool, she looked flushed and shaken. Her voice quavered, too.

But her low voice caught him like a hook right down in the gut. Damn.

"I was looking for you. I got your message and just happened to be driving by the neighborhood, so I thought I'd give it a shot. I was just about to leave when you arrived." He grinned. "Pleasant coincidence."

Her friend, Jude, had climbed out and was now peering at him over the roof of her car with an assessing, not quite friendly gaze.

"Coincidence. Right." Jude came around the car. "Cat just had a bit of a scare, so we were just coming home to batten the hatches and keep our heads down." She stood protectively by Cat and looked him up and down.

Cat's look of surprised pleasure at his presence faded into uncertainty. She glanced at her house and nodded. "I really should get inside, but I've got your syringe in the kitchen."

She led down the walkway and let herself inside. Jude stayed at the door, as if to keep Sy from entering.

"She's very afraid of something," he said.

Jude cocked a brow at him. "What makes you think that?"

He looked her square in the eyes. "The way she doesn't like to leave the house. The fear in her eyes. What happened to her?"

Jude studied his face. "What makes you think something happened?"

"People aren't born afraid. It usually takes some asshole to make them that way. Pardon my language."

Jude dropped her gaze. "It's not my story to tell. Let's just say she has good reasons, okay? I just wish—I wish I could help her over it. That's why I'm here. I'd like to see her take her life back."

"What's with all the soft voices?" Cat asked as she returned from the kitchen. She carried a ziplock bag with his syringe carefully deposited inside, but looked from Jude to Sy. Then she put hands to hips. "Let me guess. Talking about me again?" She gave Jude an evil eye, then turned the same baleful look on Sy.

"I do not take well to people talking about me behind my back. Here's your syringe. How's my big cat?"

Accepting the ziplock bag, Sy nodded. "She's awake and eating. The vet said it looked like she got in one hell of a fight with something much bigger. A bear—maybe a grizzly. Anyway, with her injured leg she couldn't hunt and was basically starving to death. With food she should live, though the vet's not too sure that front leg will ever be right again."

She sighed, but he read her relief at the news the cougar would live.

"Can—can I visit her?"

Jude looked surprised, then masked her expression.

Cat looked at Sy expectantly.

"Oh. Sure. Of course you can visit. Like I said before, we're open to the public; and once the animals are healthy, they go out into larger pens. If I'm there when you come, I'll make sure you get in to see her. Maybe give me a shout before you come."

Jude's mouth twitched at the corner as she looked between Cat and him. "Would you like to come in for a cup of tea?"

Cat brightened and nodded, but hadn't he already decided that this was a bad idea? He shook his head. "Nah. I've taken up enough of your time and I've got what I came for." He held up the syringe and backed down the porch step. "Thanks for saving it and giving me a shout. Hope to see you at the refuge some time."

He turned and strode up the walk to his truck and climbed

inside feeling a little breathless. He hadn't felt this way since he was a very young man. He started the truck, but to his surprise, Cat still stood in the doorway and waved goodbye. He could swear her friend Jude was smirking beside her.

―――――

Back at Wild Heart Refuge, the sun glittered through the tops of the tall pine, hemlock, and cedars. The air smelled of cedar, thick forest loam, and animal scat. Thankfully, the trees around the buildings kept the place cool in the summer and protected from the worse of the winter storms that could roll through from November to February. The sound of a hose said that Jana, his office manager, had taken time off from her inside duties to hose out the animal cages of the convalescing animals, something he, or a volunteer, usually did. On a hot day like today, it kept the cages clean and the animals appreciated the cool water. But he'd been too busy running after big brown eyes and a quirky smile. Hades, forgive him.

The refuge buildings were a series of log sheds with cages spread like wings to either side, a log administration building that housed the front office, a meeting room that doubled as his office, and a fully equipped veterinary exam room and surgery. All of it had been funded through donations and money that he had earned over the long years between when he was released from Hades' kingdom and now. It was amazing what a person could accumulate without trying too hard if you knew you had millennia for items to increase in value. The sale of a single original Rembrandt that he had bought out of pity when the artist was a youngster had allowed him to purchase the land and set up shop. Of course, there was no telling whether Hades would drag him back to the underworld—hadn't Persephone said Sisyphus had other things to learn, though he couldn't quite recall what they were? There were times that dreams of Persephone speaking words that he couldn't quite hear left him in a dead sweat in the night. Just how long would they give him, and if they wanted him to improve in some way, why wipe his memory of what it was? But then, there was no accounting for the ways of gods and goddesses.

Sighing, he climbed out of the truck and followed the sound of the hose, taking the syringe with him as proof that he'd absconded for a purpose. He went through the gate marked private where the concrete was damp from hosing and pushed inside the bird shed. The scent of feathers and cold water on warm concrete permeated the air. The place was dimly lit to accommodate the nocturnal birds currently housed here. The shed had a ten-foot ceiling and each of the ten cages had natural perches and access to covered external cages as well. These birds were either unable to fly or not ready to try their wings, so their space was relatively small. When they were ready, they'd be moved to larger quarters that would allow them to relearn to fly.

At the far end of the shed, caught in the angled light through the other door, a slim figure sluiced water from a hose across the floor. Jana was diminutive, with a head of scalding red hair wild enough that sometimes he was surprised that she didn't topple over with the weight of it. She usually wore the mass of curls in a tight coil wrapped like a crown around her head, but he'd seen them down a time or two. Her hair reached her knees. She wore a blue t-shirt and green cut-off dungarees so that she looked like she was about six years old, but Jana was tough.

The product of a broken home and an alcoholic single mother, she'd grown up a fighter and with an amazingly wicked sense of humor. When she saw him, she raised the hose nozzle and sprayed him head to foot.

"Shit!" He stumbled back and heard her brazen cackle. It never ceased to amaze him that such a big, gut-level laugh came from such a small woman.

"Yeah. It is and I'm hosing it because someone else played

hooky." Her no-nonsense voice filled the shed. She'd moved to the Coast about six years back and had shown up on the shelter doorstep asking for a job exactly when Sy had been considering hiring someone. She'd been with him ever since.

"I wasn't playing hooky, but I'm sorry. If you'll lower your weapon, I will assume my duties."

Jana harrumphed, but the spraying stopped and she raised the nozzle head in a salute. Of course when he started down the aisle, she couldn't resist spraying him one more time.

Spluttering, he grabbed the hose from her. "You know I'm your boss, right?" he said, fingering the nozzle trigger thoughtfully. Revenge was always sweet...

"I heard a rumor..." Her thick red tresses coiled around her shoulders like Medusa's snakes. She tapped her sneakered toe and glared her dare up at him.

One fingered, he held the nozzle up, dangling in surrender. "Okay. I admit it. I was playing hooky. For the first time, I would like to point out. And I had a reason, so it wasn't really hooky."

That was his story and he was sticking to it.

"Really? So, what was so gosh-darn important that you couldn't do your chores first?"

"You sound like my mom." He grinned down at her, knowing that was the way to get under her skin. At thirty-five, she was starting to get sensitive about getting older. "I had to pick up a syringe."

He produced the zip lock bag and she folded her arms across her chest, looking him up and down. "Interesting. Not the syringe, but the fact that you'd drive all the way into town to pick it up. That's the one from the cougar, right? Wasn't the voice message from a woman?" She glanced cagily up at him.

"I accidentally left it at the cougar rescue this morning. I thought I'd save her the trouble of bringing it here."

Both Jana's brows rose. "Save *her* the trouble, but leave *me* to clean the cages?" Then her lips quirked. "Now that *is* interesting."

She smirked at him, patted his shoulder, and then turned and left him with the hose and a half-clean aviary shed. He stuck the syringe back in his pocket and finished the job, then checked on each of the birds. The young barn owl still looked sickly and wasn't growing new feathers the way Sy would have liked him to. He was sitting in the shadowy corner of the enclosure, avoiding contact with anyone as best as he could. Sy could relate. Sometimes it was simply better to avoid contact than take the risk that human interaction could bring.

His kidding with Jana was at least safe. But with Cat Moore?

He was pretty sure it wasn't the same. In fact, he was pretty sure what he was feeling was the riskiest form of attraction. Not quite the lusty need-want he'd been driven by the first time he was alive, but something more troubling that hit him deep in his chest.

It shouldn't be possible given he'd just met the woman. He had to be imagining the feelings.

He headed for the main building where the cougar would be housed until the vet thought the cat no longer needed medication. Inside the rear door, the scent of antiseptic and animal fear filled his nose. It was something about vet offices that terrified animals, and no matter the pheromone sprays used, it couldn't be cleared. The cougar's cage was in a separate room from the surgical area to allow the animal to grow accustomed to the strange confinement.

As if that was possible.

But at least the cat wouldn't be agitated by too much stimulation. Sy went to the viewing window that looked onto the other room. Two high-set windows were the only thing providing light and the room was bathed in shadows. The cougar lay on its side, but then suddenly stirred as if it sensed someone watching. Its huge yellow-green eyes were black in the dim light, its teardrop markings vivid. Its round, black ears perked forward toward Sy. Then it turned and ran a tongue along its wrapped injured leg. The wrappings wouldn't last long if the animal grew determined to take them off, but the fact the cat was interested was a great improvement from what Sy had found in Cat's yard.

There was hope.

Satisfied, he left the vet area and went out front to the office, girding himself because he had to face Jana. Given her smirk when she handed him the hose, there was no question that he was going to get a grilling.

5

The next day dawned bright and full of promise, but then during the summer the skies were generally always sunny, and when there was rain, it was warm. At least it seemed that way to Cat when she stood on the rear deck for her daily "practice" in going outside. The breeze was light in her hair and on her skin. The peach-and-amber silk robe that she'd bought years ago in Thailand pressed softly against her skin as she watched the colors come into the world with the sun's rising. Far out on the water, tugboats hauled barge-loads of shipping containers up the coast. Others hauled gravel to the building industry down south. Later would come the sailboats with their white spinnaker sails belling into the wind. And far across the water, the windows of Nanaimo caught the sun. As she sipped her coffee and inhaled the sweet ocean air, the soft tread of Jude's footsteps came from the house behind her.

There truly was something special about this place, this landscape. The twisted red trunk and the glossy green leaves of the arbutus tree in the stony corner of the yard was one of the most beautiful things she'd ever seen. It was one of the reasons she'd bought the house. The tree was contorted and twisted but it was strong. Sort of like the cougar was wounded, but the cat hadn't given up yet.

Her thoughts ranged to the quiet confidence Sy Foster had shown as he worked with the animal. It was the same quiet confidence that had got her out of her house to help him. He was a good-looking man with those Mediterranean dark eyes of his and those strong, tanned arms and legs. Not super tall, but tall enough. She wondered if he was always that confident.

"Penny?" Jude said coming up beside her smelling of floral shower gel. Her brown hair fluffed around her head as the breeze dried it.

Cat swallowed back her embarrassment at being caught thinking of a guy. "Just how I love this place. It's magical. I feel calm when I look at it." Her words came out wistful, even to her.

"I understand there're lots of places to see on the Sunshine Coast. Nice walks and so on. I think we should go do some while I'm here."

Cat closed her eyes, all the serene joy of the morning sucked away.

"You have to do that, do you? Make your visit all about healing me? What if I'm happy the way I am? What if I need to take my own time to heal? Healing's not something you do on command, you know." She turned to face Jude.

"Seriously? You're going to try that on me?" Jude set her coffee down as if it had gone bad. "It's been two years, Cat. Two years—and you've gotten worse, not better. That's not healing, that's giving up!"

Cat looked away, back out to the water and the first early sailboat cruising up the coast before the wind. Once upon a time she'd thought about learning to sail and going around the world. Fat chance now.

"Maybe this wasn't a good idea, you coming here for the week," she said softly. Her chest hurt. Through everything, Jude had been her greatest friend, her staunchest ally in getting on her feet again. They'd celebrated each milestone together as Cat's condition improved and she *had* improved physically.

But Jude didn't seem able to accept that Cat had plateaued— that this was as good as it was going to get.

"Maybe it was exactly the right thing to happen. I mean, Jeezus, Cat, you imagined you saw Kyle Redburn yesterday! You've let your fear rule you so long that the moment you step outside you find a reason to run back home again!"

Cat whirled around. "You don't believe that I saw him. You think I'm crazy! Poor ol' Cat has locked herself away so long she's gone off her rocker! Is that it?" Her hands balled to fists and her voice had risen so her neighbors could probably hear, but she was done with letting other people tell her what was good for her. "You know what? This wasn't a good idea at all. I think you should leave and I don't think you should come again until you can accept me the way I am."

She turned her back on Jude and stared out at the ocean, hugging herself.

"Cat no. Please."

Cat refused to answer. Friends were supposed to love you for what and who you were—not try to change you.

Jude sighed behind her. "All right. I'll make us some breakfast and then I'll head for the next ferry."

"I'm not hungry." Cat shook her head and looked at her watch. "The next ferry's in fifty minutes. If you leave now, you can make it."

There was no response except footfall across the deck, the sound of movement in the house, and then the too-final click of the front door closing. What was she doing? Jude was her friend! For the past two years Jude had been her one constant relationship. Just about everyone else had drifted away because of Cat's refusal to leave her house.

The sound of a car engine starting jarred her into action. She didn't want Jude to go. She was acting like a spoiled brat. She needed Jude's friendship. The human contact.

Cat left her cup balanced on the porch railing and dashed for the front door. Threw it open and leapt down the stairs, but the blue car had disappeared down the hill to the highway and she was standing here exposed at the side of the street. A gasp of pain escaped her and then the panic set in. She scrambled back to the house, slammed the door and locked it behind her, then leaned against its solid wood, because she didn't think she could move anymore.

Her knees gave and she slid down to sit on her heels.

What had she done? It was as if she'd picked a fight with Jude simply because Jude had pointed out what was obvious. Cat was becoming a shut-in.

Becoming, like heck.

Jude was right. She *was* a shut-in. And she'd done it to herself by giving into her fear.

———

An hour later she'd showered and dressed in denim capris and blue-and-white striped t-shirt and had tried again and again to reach Jude by phone to apologize and beg her to come back, but her friend's phone either wasn't working or she wasn't picking up. Most likely the latter. Cat had really done it this time. With her parents having passed, Jude had been the one good thing Cat had held onto from her former life. Yes, she had a brother and sister, but her brother was busy with his career and his wife and had no time for a shut-in sister. Get over it, he'd say.

Her older sister was simply unavailable, working half a world away at a resort in the former Yugoslavia.

And now Cat had alienated Jude. She felt like crying, but that was giving up. In the old days she'd have driven over to Jude's house to apologize and fix things. This time it was a little more difficult. Not only did Cat have to leave her house, she'd have to take the ferry over to the mainland and then drive all the way out the Fraser Valley to Langley.

Just the thought of that length of time outside her house and having to interact with so many people left her in a cold sweat. Not to mention returning to the community where Kyle Redburn had attacked her.

The question was what was she going to do about it?

Darn it all, Kyle Redburn had beaten her physically. It didn't mean that she had to stay beaten. Jude was probably right—Cat had allowed her fear and imagination to merge and that had led to her thinking she saw him at the grocery store. It was simply too big a coincidence for it to be real.

So, if she had nothing to fear, why was she holding herself confined to the house?

She grabbed her purse and, on impulse, the card that Sy Foster had left her. It had been almost twenty-four hours since he rescued the cougar. She could drive to his center and maybe he'd allow her to visit the animal. He had a nice smile, Sy did. It might be nice to see him again.

Decided, she headed for the door into the garage. It felt strange stepping through the doorway because she'd had little reason to do so given she hadn't been going anywhere for the past few months. The scent of car oil and gasoline tanged the air. She stabbed the button for the automatic door opener, climbed into her silver Prius, and started the engine, then backed out of the garage.

The sunlight through the windshield and the moon roof felt blinding. She fumbled in her glove box for sunglasses and hauled them on. She was already sweating and the car wasn't hot. What the heck had she done confining herself like that?

Well, no more!

She backed up the driveway and onto the street and sat there breathing hard as the garage door slid down, trying to slow her racing heart. It didn't work, but it would have to calm down eventually, because she was not giving up. She had fences to mend with Jude, and in the meantime, a cougar to visit.

She punched the Wild Heart Refuge address into her GPS and waited for the machine to compute. Then she set out, following directions.

Don't stop. Don't hesitate or she'd turn the car around and head home again.

The drive took her north to the edge of the town of Sechelt and then she turned away from Davis Bay toward Porpoise Bay on the other side of the peninsula that joined to the mainland at Sechelt. Through a light industrial area where the traffic was thankfully light, but her sweat was coming harder, her shirt sticking to her back, her hair turning stringy. In the rearview mirror, her face was flushed and she was puffing as if she'd run a race.

Too bad. She was doing this. She was going to follow the directions even though fear was making it harder to think. But she was doing this.

She *was!*

Out past the turnoff sign for the city dump. Out past the attractive carved wood signs to Porpoise Bay Provincial Park. Over a small river. The GPS told her that her turn was coming eight hundred meters ahead.

She slowed and a small green-and-gold sign with a stylized owl figure, its breast filled with a broad heart, announced Wild Heart Conservancy and Animal Refuge. She swung the Prius onto the dirt road.

It sloped steeply uphill away from the water, the road filled with potholes filled with gravel, so the Prius seemed to lose traction from time to time. On either side of the car, the cedar and pine trees grew taller, with sunlight filtered dimly through their crowns to spotlight fallen giants and clumps of ferns.

The road crested the slope and the trees seemed to gather as the road widened into a parking lot. Ahead, a low-slung log building was flanked by a variety of structures that straggled up the hill amongst the trees. Some were the same log construction as the main building, but others were of plank boards now graying with age. She slid the Prius into an empty parking spot and sat there, still fighting to slow her breathing. There was a small red Toyota parked in front of the main building, but otherwise no sign of life.

Maybe this was a bad idea. Sy hadn't looked like a small red Toyota kinda guy. No, trucks like the one from yesterday were more his style. So Sy wasn't here.

She couldn't deny her disappointment.

But she'd come this far. She was not leaving without at least seeing the cougar.

She closed her eyes and inhaled, then pushed the driver's side door open. Her hands shook. So did her knees.

The scent of cedar and pine flooded her nose. The soft hush of the wind in the trees was sublime and for a moment she almost felt like weeping for the peace the place evoked. Slowly, the shaking subsided and she stretched her arms out to either side and turned her face to the sun, then raised her arms overhead almost as if she was worshipping.

Maybe she was. It was as if the tension that had ridden her chest for so long suddenly eased. It wasn't gone, but in this place, just as in her house, she could breathe. All the tight knotting in her neck and shoulders began to give.

A door opened and closed behind her and boots crunched on gravel.

She whirled around and found herself facing a petite woman with a red crown that caught the sunlight like copper. Not a crown. A thick braid of red hair coiled around the crown of her head. A light spatter of freckles dotted her tanned, slightly upturned nose. She wore a red-and-white t-shirt under a pair of faded-green denim cutoffs.

"Can I help you?" she asked. Her voice was throaty and warm. "We're closed right now, but our public tours will run this afternoon."

"Are you Jana?" Cat took a stab in the dark.

The red head's gaze narrowed suspiciously. "What if I am?"

Cat shook her head. "Nothing, really. I just heard your name on your voice mail when I left a message for Sy. I'm Cat Moore."

Jana's gaze rounded and so did her mouth. She gave Cat a quick once-over. "Of course. You're the syringe message." The little moue of her mouth suggested there was something she left unsaid.

For some reason Cat felt herself color. "Guilty. Sy left the syringe at my place so I wanted to make sure it was returned."

Jana just looked at her as if sizing her up.

"He picked it up yesterday," said Cat.

Jana nodded slowly. Her arms crossed over her chest. "What can we do for you, now?"

"Well—uh—" The tension was back. Sweat poured down Cat's back under Jana's stare. "I came up to see the cougar, but now that I've seen this place I'm wondering—do you accept volunteers?"

What the heck was she doing? She'd barely been able to make it out of the house today. Who knew if she could even walk or stand without the Prius' solid support behind her. Now she thought she could volunteer? But, strangely, there was something about this place that felt, well, safe, even if Jana wasn't the most welcoming.

Jana frowned. "We do. We have a training program for volunteers to work with the animals, but we just ran one and another doesn't start for four weeks."

Suddenly it was very important that she do this. If she didn't commit to something now, Cat seriously doubted that she'd make it out of the house again.

"Please. I'll do anything. It doesn't have to be with the animals although I'd love to work with them. I'll pick weeds, clean stalls or whatever you house the animals in. Whatever you need. I just need—I need a purpose."

As she said it, she realized it was true. All her working career as a probation officer she'd had victims and criminals who were her responsibility. Now she had nothing—not even a pet.

Jana's brow rose as if questioning Cat's sanity. She had every right to wonder. Cat looked down at her drenched top and swiped at the sweat on her face.

"Listen, I've not been well for a long time. I was off on medical leave from work and I've realized that I need to be doing again. Anything." She looked up at the trees again overwhelmed by the magical feel of the place. "This place—I know I just got here, but it's special just like the Sunshine Coast is special. It—it fills you up, you know?"

Jana doubtful expression softened slightly. "Most people just ask to see the animals. They don't appreciate the trees." She shook her head. "These days it seems like all anyone wants to do is cut them down for the view. We'd have a view here, too, if we cut down these beauties." She lifted her chin back the way Cat had driven in.

Cat looked the way Jana motioned and through the trees along the road she glimpsed bits of ocean blue—Porpoise Bay.

"I—I have a view at my place and I love it, but it's not like this. This—it feels like something living!" She felt herself blushing. This woman must think Cat was a ninny. Of course, the forest was alive. "Anyway, I'm willing to do whatever needs doing. I'm fairly strong and I'm willing to work."

Jana cocked her hip and tapped her chin with her finger as she considered Cat's request. Finally, she nodded. "All right. Our illustrious leader seems to have a broken alarm clock today and there're sheds that need cleaning." She looked Cat up and down. "You're not exactly dressed for work…"

Cat looked down at her capris, blue-and-white striped t-shirt, and the pristine white sneakers on her feet. "Everything's washable." And what wasn't she could always replace. Online shopping was good for that.

With a gleam in her eye, Jana led off to a shed at the rear of the compound of structures.

"This is our bat cage." Jana's lips edged up in a grin. "That's cage, not cave; and no, there is no Clive Owen wannabe inside. The bats here on the Sunshine Coast are facing the same issues as bats everywhere—loss of habitat, pollution, and a fungus infection that's been killing off whole colonies. These guys were babies, rescued when an old house was pulled down and their parents abandoned them. We've opened the eaves so they could leave and join an existing colony, and there's a cave back in the hills from here where we carried them before releasing, but they came back and seem to have moved in to stay. They come and go as they please. Their new colony. There's a couple of UBC researchers who have tagged them."

She opened the shed door, releasing the pungent scent of bat guano, and stepped inside into almost darkness. Cat followed her in.

The air was surprisingly warm given it was still cool outside under the trees. They stood in almost darkness in a narrow corridor between two mesh walls that created two enclosures that filled either side of the shed from one end to the other. The air was filled with soft rustlings and squeaks that made the little hairs on Cat's neck stand on end. When she sought the source high up in the enclosures, a mass of moving something was clustered along a maze of perches in the ceiling rafters. The concrete floors at the base of the cage were a mess of smeary gray and black blotches.

Skin crawling, she jerked back her explorations and focused

on Jana. The red head had found a hose attached to a faucet at the rear of the shed across from the one door.

"Like this," Jana said. She turned on the tap and trained the hose nozzle on the floor of the cage on the right. A torrent of water blasted across the floor, peeling back the guano. Jana hosed it toward a drain at the outside edge of the rear of the building. Then she closed the nozzle. "You try."

Cat accepted the hose and aimed at the cage floor. A massive spray rebounded at her and Jana. Jana sprang out of the way, avoiding the worst of it, but Cat's capris were soaked and spattered with debris and her sneakers were suddenly gray.

"Keep the angle like this!" Jana leapt in and forced Cat's hands down. The torrent of water stopped spraying and the guano on the cage floor peeled away.

"That's it. You've got it. Now finish this cage and then call me. I'll be in the front office."

The door to the bat cage shed opened and closed, leaving Cat alone with a spraying hose and two cages full of bats and guano. Her eyes grew accustomed to the dim light so that she could see the bats swarmed overhead. They peered down at her with small bright eyes or hid their faces under leathery wings. Not so scary after all.

She kept hosing, sheeting the debris toward the drain. A couple of times she mistakenly sprayed too close to the wall and sent a wave of water sluicing back over the cage floor, into the corridor and her no longer pristine shoes. She was almost done when the shed door opened behind her and a figure blocked the sunlight.

Jana come to check on her, so Cat had probably taken far too much time and water to get the job done. But done it was. Without turning to Jana, she turned off the water and coiled the hose.

"All done," she said. "I hope it's up to your standards." She turned around.

Sy Foster leaned against the doorframe, a strange mix of humor and admiration on his face.

She took an involuntary step backward. "You! I thought it was Jana!"

"Not Jana." He stepped into the shed and the door bumped closed behind him, cutting off the light. "What are you doing here, Cat?" In the dim interior his voice was soft and his gaze seemed hot on her skin, but he left the length of the shed between them.

"Volunteering, of course." She grinned to keep the embarrassment off her face. She must look a sight all soaked and filthy, but if that came with the territory, she could handle it. The man before her, she wasn't as sure of. "I needed to get out of the house so I came up hoping to see the cougar, but when I got here —well..." She shrugged. "I really like your refuge."

And maybe that was what it was—Wild Heart Refuge might be messy, but it felt like a refuge for her, too.

6

____

Cat Moore was dripping and filthy standing there at the back of the bat shed, but her face positively glowed. The meagre light reflecting off the wet concrete seemed to catch in her brown eyes and on her skin so that she was different, a fey creature of magic and fully alive.

Sy blinked. What the hell was he on about? Even hosed out, the shed was smelly, yet he could still catch the scent of apples and roses he'd noticed the other day. And he could swear he felt the heat off her body in the cool air.

He pulled his gaze from her wide eyes and the damp t-shirt that hinted at what was underneath, and looked at the cages. The floors were as clean as they had ever been. "Looks like a good job. You should even pass Jana's inspection." He took another step toward her and stopped himself. Yes. Roses and green apples and maybe a hint of strawberry, too. She smelled of summer.

He stuck his hands in his pockets. "You, on the other hand, look like you could use a shower and a change of clothes. You should have worn the boots and coveralls."

"Boots?" She looked puzzled.

"There're a few pairs we wear for these jobs," he said and sighed. "Let me guess. Jana didn't offer them to you."

"Well, no, but I was kind of pushy and insistent. Like I said. I came up here and I didn't want to leave so I told her I wanted to volunteer. She gave me this as a job." She looked down at herself and looked a little dismayed. "I guess coveralls and boots would have been a good idea."

He nodded. "Come on. Let's get you out of here to somewhere you might dry out."

Backing up, he held the door for her and nearly touched her back as she preceded him out. But something stopped him and he wasn't sure whether it was something about her—that wariness he'd seen before—or fear for himself. There was something about Cat Moore that was so damned attractive, from her sweaty chin-length blonde hair to her filthy once-had-been-white sneakers. Regardless of the externals, there was a real beating heart there and—and the woman whose chest it was in was wounded.And apparently unaware of the effect she had on him.

Sure, he might want to protect her from whatever had her scared of living, but there was more, too. A stirring he hadn't felt since long before the eons spent pushing a boulder up a hill.

He led her past the other sheds, pointing out the raptor and owl shed, the one reserved for nocturnal animals like possum and raccoon, and another building in a large pen where a small group of deer grazed on hay set out for them.

Spotlighted in dappled sunlight, a mother deer with a healing leg allowed twin spotted fawns to nurse.

"Beautiful,"Cat breathed as if she was afraid to disturb the scene.

"She could barely stand when she was found. We think she might have been hit by a car. The fawns were starving. We managed to catch all three and bring them in. They should be ready to be released in the fall."

"What a wonderful way to live your life. Saving all these

magnificent creatures," Cat said. She was looking up at him with something almost akin to awe.

He had to look away. After all he'd done in his existence, he certainly didn't deserve any praise. "It's—right. The right thing to do."

He nodded her away from the pen toward the administration building because he couldn't afford for anyone to admire him. Admiration went too easily to one's head. He knew that all too well.

Inside the front office, meditative music and the comforting tap-tap-tap of Jana's typing filled the air. It was a good place. The log walls gave the rooms a warm, golden glow. The place filled the broad front of the building with a seated waiting area, a couple of displays of Wild Heart Refuge items for sale, and a postcard display. On the walls were a map of the Sunshine Coast and a couple of water color paintings of old-growth forests.

The room was simply furnished with a desk and computer for Jana and a table that held a tangle of houseplants that threw up shoots, leaves, and flowers in profusion. Two doors sat side-by-side in the back wall, one leading to his small office-meeting room and the other giving onto the veterinary clinic.

Jana looked up from her typing. Her gaze brightened when she saw him. "Sy. Hi. You were missed this morning." Then her gaze caught on the bedraggled-looking figure accompanying him and her smile diminished slightly. "I see you found Cat. She wanted—wants—to volunteer."

"And that is very kind of her."

"Yeah. So, I hadn't gotten to the bat cage yet so I set her up and showed her how."

"Uh huh." He nodded and gave Cat a little nudge forward, so the full impact of the ravages of her labor were evident beyond the squelching of her shoes on the vinyl-tiled floor. "Has she filled in the paperwork yet?"

Jana looked down at her desk. "Uh, no. But I have it here ready for her."

She picked up a pen and offered it to Cat. Cat squelched forward, took the pen, and pulled the form to her.

"She looks a little the worse for wear," Sy said. "I thought we bought a bunch of coveralls and boots for cleaning out the buildings."

He said nothing more, just watched the slow flush run up Jana's shoulders, neck, and face. She looked away. "I'm sorry. I guess it was an oversight. Cat was so eager…"

Cat glanced up from filling out the form. "It's really not a problem. It was great to get out of the house and see the animals. I was hoping I might get to see my friend the cougar. How is she doing?"

"She's still in the clinic, but she's doing pretty well. She's actually up and moving around her cage a little. That bodes well." Sy grinned down at her. "I can't take you into her cage room, but I can let you see her."

Jana cocked a brow at him, her lips in a line. Sy chose to ignore her expression and led Cat, sopping feet and all, back through the door to the veterinary clinic. At the observation window that gave onto the cage room, he stopped and Cat came up beside him.

"She's there."

Cat stepped closer to the window, her hand coming up to almost touch the glass. But she didn't touch, caught herself, and dropped her hand to her side. She was very much in control of her body.

In the cage room, the cougar was standing in her cage peering out at them, her black muzzle and the teardrop black markings on her face emphasizing her tawny gold coat and green-gold eyes. Her long tail flicked at the black tip; her side was marred with the still livid wounds. As they watched, the animal looked away as if sensing no threat and settled herself on her belly. The leg bandage removed, she began licking the healing marks on her leg and side.

Cat sighed as if she'd been holding her breath. "She is so beautiful."

"She's a top predator, just like us."

She frowned. "I guess it is better to see things as they really are. Yes, she's graceful and gorgeous, but she wouldn't be good to run into alone in the woods. She's wild."

Sy nodded.

"You know, you really didn't have to give Jana a hard time. I asked her to let me do something. She told me about the training, but I pushed her to let me do something immediately." She looked ashamed. "I got out here and I just couldn't go home again. It took too much effort to get out the door in the first place. And then I saw the trees."

He wasn't quite certain he understood, but she saved him from responding.

"I guess I should get home and have a shower. This really isn't my best look." She grinned up at him and it was like a wash of sunlight through the clouds.

He caught her shoulders. "Next time you come up, make sure you get the boots and coveralls. That's your first lesson in caring for the animals."

She nodded up at him, far too close for comfort and yet he left his hands on her shoulders and she didn't duck out of them.

"Coveralls. Check. Books. Check." She saluted with a little laugh and then patted the back of his right hand. "Thank you for putting up with a wild woman barging into your refuge."

She ducked past him just as he was going to nudge a strand of hair behind her ear. At the door to the front office, she stopped. "You know, it really feels like a refuge, but for people, too."

Then she was gone through the door, leaving him feeling stunned. He heard female laughter and then silence. Through the observation window,he saw that the female cougar had stretched out and laid her head on her paws. She was looking at him as if she really saw him and he couldn't help but wonder just how deep inside him she looked. Cat's last glance over her shoulder had been oddly similar. How had she known this place was his refuge after a lifetime of searching for, and failing to find, redemption?

The better question was what did her awareness mean?

With a last glance at the cat, he went back into the front office. Jana was typing again, but her steady tap-tap-tap faltered when he entered.

"I apologize. It was stupid, petty, juvenile behavior on my part," she said. "It won't happen again." She crossed her heart.

"Good. We don't do that to our volunteers. They work from the goodness of their hearts. They—she—deserve better." He headed for his office.

Jana angled her head. "Sorry, Boss. This one's different somehow, isn't she?"

He stopped and turned to her. "What does that mean?"

Her brows lifted and her lips curved in a knowing grin. "Maybe you should tell me. First you drive all the way to her place for no valid reason."

"The syringe…"

She held up ahand to stop his protest. "First the special trip and now you sort of rescue her from the bat cave and give her a personal guided tour to the animal of her choice. That's very different from how you treat your other acolytes. And then there's the way you look at her—like you are sort of stunned and puzzled at the same time."

He rolled his gaze heavenward. "How many times do I have to tell you that I don't have acolytes, and to remind you that any extra women we have hanging around here are more or less your doing? You're the one who keeps trying to set me up, even though I've told you that I'm not interested. Cat's no different from all the others."

He scowled at her and she burst out laughing.

"Right; and you've never protested like this either. Sounds to me like you really might be off the market this time," she said.

Millennia ago he'd have killed anyone who laughed at him. This time round he liked the laughter better.

Even if he felt his own flush heating up his face because something about Cat Moore was definitely different.

————

It was the next morning when he realized exactly how different Cat Moore was. There it was, eight thirty in the morning, and his truck had somehow found its way to the parking spot along the road at the front of Cat's house. Eight thirty, and the dew was still weighting the pink rose petals in front of the house next door. Eight thirty, and through his open window came the trill of a towhee in Cat's overgrown front garden, the shrill of the flicker woodpecker in the pines growing up beside her house, and the not-too-distant cry of a bald eagle from down near the shoreline. Underneath the bird call and the sounds of the two lanes of Sunshine Coast Highway traffic down in Davis Bay came the wind in the trees and the sound of ocean. It was a soft roar that filled the life of people who lived on the Coast, as if the ocean purred for them, comforting them and telling them they were home.

At least that was what he had felt when he came here. Funny, all those years as king of Ephyra, what was now known as Corinth, and he had never noticed such a thing in the seas around his homeland. Either the ocean here was different or he was a different man. Perhaps it was the latter.

That explained his attraction to the Sunshine Coast, but what was his excuse for being here?

Had he really come just to check on her and apologize for what had happened yesterday at the refuge?

Sure. And after all the long years of his existence he was now able to fly like a pig.

Sighing, he punched the steering wheel once and opened the truck door to step outside. Who was he kidding? Certainly not himself after a long night of tossing and turning and rethinking how he had dealt with Cat yesterday. That was not like him.

He'd been a king, dammit. Everyone had done his bidding and darn well liked it. They hadn't dared to laugh at him behind his back and definitely not to his face as Jana had. His fists curled, but then he sighed again. After millennia toiling at the most futile of labors, he was no longer a king. Ephyra was no more and the refuge was no kingdom. He was a man. Only a man who was trying to leave the world a slightly better place than he'd found it this second time around. He was a man who found himself attracted to Cat Moore, more than he cared to be.

But this incarnation was all about stewardship for the land and the animals. Not getting his own needs met.

Cat's front door swung open and there she was, looking sleepy and newly showered, with her blonde hair still wet and sleeked back from her smooth brow. She wore white shorts and a pink sleeveless top that swung around her hips. No makeup that he could tell and she looked fresh and alive and eminently attractive with those long legs and arms of hers exposed. He caught himself wondering whether she had tan lines.

She sipped a cup of coffee and eyed him as if uncertain whether she should return inside and lock the door behind her or stay where she was. She nodded and her throat worked.

"Imagine my surprise when I looked out my front window. There's another chair on the back deck and a cup with your name on it if you want to come in." Her voice came out a little hoarse. She cleared her throat and grinned at him.

"It must have surprised you to see I was here," he said, and started down the walk to the house.

"Surprised." She sniffed and seemed to force a chuckle. "That's one way to put it."

He stopped midstride. "Listen, I can come back if this isn't a good time."

"No." She shook her head. "This is a good time. In fact, it's a great time." She seemed to take a deep breath as if steeling herself and then she stepped aside to let him inside. He climbed the three stairs to her front door.

He looked down at her and then stepped into the hall, hearing a small catch in her breath as if his presence surprised her. With a quick scan of the street, she closed the door behind her and turned to him.

"Welcome to my home. Thank you for coming."

More formal than he would have expected. He followed her from the front door to the well-laid-out kitchen-dining-living area that filled the back of the house. A bank of windows gave onto an expansive view of the ocean.

She caught him looking.

"I never get tired of looking at that view," she said as she bustled behind the kitchen island and busied herself steaming milk and percolating espresso. "It's my addiction," she said when she caught him studying her. "I missed my lattes and the coffee shop culture, so I figured I could at least get the coffee so I bought the equipment." She poured both liquids into a waiting cup and came around the counter to him. "Here you go. If you want sugar, I have some in the cupboard."

"No sugar, thanks." He didn't have the heart to tell her that he didn't exactly care for the modern "frilly" drinks. Foam. No foam. Decaf. Cinnamon. Sprinkles. Give him a cup of plain black coffee. To be polite, he sipped.

The milky froth on the top was sweet counterpoint to the extra strong coffee underneath. It tasted of earth and oils and nut kernels and was more full-bodied than anything he'd ever tasted. The brew Jana made at the office was suddenly downright insipid.

"What. Is. This?" He held the amazing cup up between them.

The sunlight through the bank of windows seemed to find her face so that she positively beamed at him.

"Actually, it's my own special blend of beans. With steamed milk, of course." She clinked mugs with him. "I'm glad you like it. Would you like to sit in here or outside?"

"Outside, I'm thinking. It's a gorgeous day. Did you see the rainbows over Vancouver Island this morning?"

"I did." Momentary pleasure crossed her face. "It wasn't a whole rainbow because of the clouds. More like someone had strung pieces of rainbows like beads across the top of the water. Very pretty." Then she frowned. "But that was over an hour ago and you couldn't have seen them from the refuge. Do you live around here?"

He hid his faux pas in another sip of coffee and shook his head. "I guess I'm—what's the word?—busted? I was sitting outside in my truck."

"For an hour?"

He felt unfamiliar embarrassment again. "More like an hour and a half."

She set her cup down and her hands on her hips. "For goodness sake, Sy. Don't you know what a doorbell is? You could have let me know you were here. I was up."

Shaking her head, she let them out onto the deck; yet the way her knuckles whitened momentarily on the doorframe and how she seemed to suck in a deep breath as if she was a diver about to submerge suggested that being outside wasn't her favorite thing.

She motioned him to a chair and perched herself on the patio rail. "So what brings you here? I've already given you my cougar." She flushed. "The cougar. Not my cougar." She shook her head. "I think I mentioned that I'm not used to having men in my house."

Looking at her beautiful eyes and her trim figure, he figured not having men around couldn't be true and he had clearly gotten the vibe that she was as attracted to him as he was to her. He looked at the milky goodness in his cup and felt endlessly stupid. "Actually, I was going to ask you if you'd like to go out for a cup of coffee, but I've a feeling that no matter where I take you it won't measure up." He saluted her with the mug. "This is *very* good."

"After living in Vancouver, I guess I've become something of a coffee snob. I order the beans in now that I'm over here." Cat actually blushed a ridiculously attractive flush that went right down to her shoulders.

"So if not coffee, how about dinner. I'm sure I can find a tie and knock the bat guano off my shoes," he said.

Her expression turned to mock horror as she pointedly looked at his shoes.

"Don't worry. I wasn't on bat cave duty today," he said.

She sipped her coffee thoughtfully and sighed. Her flush, if anything, increased. "Thing is, Sy, I don't go out much anymore and going out at night—well, I haven't done anything like that in years—not even with friends." She shook her head. "I'm sorry. I really am."

It didn't sound like a brush off, but it sure felt that way and it was something he had never had to get used to. But he found the grace to nod. "Okay. No dinner. Lunch maybe? Or a walk on the beach?"

Damn, he sounded desperate even to himself and Cat was looking increasingly uncomfortable as if she didn't quite know how to handle a guy who kept putting himself out there. Except he hadn't put himself out there even though the ladies had come calling. He felt like a damn fool.

Hades must be roaring with laughter at how Sy was sweating.

He shook his head. "Listen, I'm out of practice with this whole boy-meets-girl thing. How about I just quit embarrassing myself and get out of here." He set down his mug only half-drunk and stood up. The breeze off the ocean tugged at his hair as if Poseidon was telling him he was making a stupid decision.

"Sy, no." She slid off the rail and stood with him. "You don't have to go. Finish your coffee and let's talk about something else. How—how long have you lived on the Coast?" It was like she was grasping for conversation.

Sit? Leave? Even though the situation wasn't what he'd planned, it was still an opportunity to get to know this woman. He scooped up his mug and went to the deck rail.

"Ten years and counting. I came up here to find the end of the road and fell in love with the air, the scenery, and the land. I bought that piece of land and the rest is history." He shrugged and turned back to her.

"Where did you move from?" she asked, her gaze bright and interested.

"Where didn't I come from?" he said. "I've been a wanderer for many years. I spent time in Southeast Asia and India. I helped sheep farm in Australia. Worked as a tour guide in Patagonia. Shrimp farmed down in the Carolinas." He shrugged. The jobs he'd mentioned had been decades apart and interspersed with too much time as a soldier fighting from the Boer war to Korea. "I spent some time as an aid worker in the former Yugoslavia, but then I came here."

"You must have needed a rest," Cat said.

"Something like that." What he'd needed was a purpose, and all those other efforts had left him no farther ahead in his search for redemption than pushing that damned boulder up a hill.

"So you've traveled a lot. Where were you from originally?"

Her question was natural, but it wasn't one he cared to answer. Still…

"My family is Greek."

Cat put her mug down. "Really? I never would have guessed. You've got exactly no accent."

"I've had time to unlearn it." He returned to the table and sat down across from her. "How about you? You said you were living in Langley. What brought you here?"

She looked away and her shoulders huddled in a little. Then she drew in a deep breath and consciously set her shoulders back. Whatever had brought her here wasn't exactly something she liked to remember—or talk about. But she nodded.

"There was an incident at work. It left me needing a break, so I sold and came here."

"Retirement?" But she was far too young for that.

She shook her head. "Worker's Compensation. I'm on pension." She smiled up at him. "But that's ancient history. Now I'm here and looking for something purposeful to get me out of the house. During the day," she amended.

And so clearly, lunch or a walk with him were not what fell into the purposeful category. He really should be going, but on the other hand there was the challenge of trying to find out exactly what made Cat Moore tick. He hadn't given up on boulder pushing and he wasn't going to give up on Cat Moore, either. There was something about her.

Something that said that, just like his animals, she, too, needed healing.

7

———————

There was no question but that Sy Foster was a handsome guy. Sitting across from Cat on this sunny day with the deep blue sky and with the sunlight caught in his dark curls, she could actually imagine sitting on the small terra cotta balcony of a white-washed house with blue domes and the glimmering Aegean Sea as the background. She could even picture him in a toga with his strong shoulders and legs exposed and tanned from a lifetime of climbing hills dotted with olive groves and flocks of sheep and shepherds. Heck, he could have been a shepherd if his family hadn't left Greece whenever they did.

She sipped her coffee and sighed at the lovely rich tannins and nuttiness of the bean, letting the warmth of the sun beat into her flesh.

"What are you thinking?" Sy asked.

"Why?" she asked, coloring slightly. Her thoughts were her own. At least that was something Kyle Redburn hadn't been able to take from her. She had her mind and her own thoughts that she didn't have to share with anyone.

"You just looked faraway. I wondered where you'd gone."

She met his dark gaze and had to sigh again. "I was thinking about Greece, if you must know. It's one of those places I've always wanted to see, but never did. Greece was always going to be there while the plains of Africa and the great herds aren't." She shook her head. "I wonder whether I'll ever make it. To Greece, I mean."

But she knew she meant far more than Greece. Living like a shut-in wasn't any life at all. The trouble was, she didn't know if she could beat it alone; and so far, Jude still hadn't returned her calls.

"What's stopping you from going?" he asked gently. He took a swig of his coffee and set the mug down.

"What isn't?" She shook her head bitterly. "Let's just say the trip is a little beyond me these days."

There was a beat of uncomfortable silence.

"When you decide to visit, I'd be happy to suggest places to go, things to see." He shoved up from the table to gaze down at her.

Thankfully, even from his greater height, she didn't feel threatened. That was unusual.

"I'd better get going. Not overstay my welcome and all that. Thanks for the coffee. It really was wonderful."

He waved off her protests and headed inside and through to the front door only to pause. "If you don't mind, I might drop around from time to time." He had the nicest of smiles when he gazed down at her. "Who knows. Maybe eventually you'll let me take you out of here. In the meantime, any time you want to come up to the refuge and help with the cage cleaning, you'll be welcome. Really."

He opened the door and hesitated, then leaned down for a brief peck on her cheek that stunned her. Then he was gone down the walk and up to his truck. He climbed in and rolled down his window, waved, and started the engine. Then he was gone.

And she still hadn't moved. The touch of his lips was like lightning and thunder echoing in her brain.

———

The sound of Sy's truck engine was long gone by the time Cat found the strength to pull herself together and close the door.

What the heck was she doing even letting the man in her door? And he'd touched her! Touched her without asking for permission! It left her heart beating so hard she could barely breathe. She snapped the lock on and closed the deadbolt, then stood there trying to catch her breath. Even the house that had been her refuge seemed dangerous. She'd invited him in and, yes, he'd been a perfect gentleman, but if he'd attacked her there was nothing she could have done. Heck, he could have killed her and no one would have known.

No one would have cared, either, now that Jude was gone.

How could Jude have been so ridiculous as to think that Cat needed to get out amongst people? How could Cat have been stupid enough to think that Jude might be right?

It was too dangerous to be out there. It might even be too dangerous to be in her house, now that Sy Foster knew where she lived. She knew almost nothing about him. He could be a rapist and murderer hiding out from police for all she knew. She'd have to sell the house and move.

No. That wasn't right.

She inhaled and slowed the wild careening of her thoughts. A man who cared for animals like Sy Foster wasn't the usual profile of rapist and murderer. Often they had a history of animal cruelty and sadistic behavior. A man who ran an animal refuge wasn't someone she'd suspect of that background.

Her mind was running wild for no reason. It was her *imagination…*

Her palm covered the spot where his lips had touched her skin. The spot still tingled. Her cheek felt warm.

When she focused only on what had happened, she realized it was a nice kiss. A gentlemanly kiss. Not a bit threatening. Almost pleasant, in fact. Pleasant enough she might like it to happen again.

Her breathing was almost back to normal as she retreated farther into the house. Sy could have tried something when she was in the bat cage, but he'd been a perfect gentleman there, too. So maybe Sy Foster wasn't a risk. Maybe it was okay to continue to volunteer at the refuge.

She sank into a blue leather chair and gazed out the broad windows. What the heck had she done to herself? She used to be brave. She used to confront convicted criminals and hold them accountable for their actions. At this moment if one of them said "boo," she'd most likely run screaming.

She didn't like feeling like this—afraid of the world.

She squared her shoulders. Tomorrow she'd go out to the refuge again and if she was sent to hose out the cages, well, she'd remember to get boots and coveralls and to take a hairbrush with her. She was *not* going to allow Kyle Redburn to beat her. Not anymore.

She smiled and wondered whether Sy had any idea of the effect he'd had on her. Talk about mood swings—terror to attraction followed by resolve to be a better person.

"Not bad, Mr. Foster. Maybe sometime I'll tell you about it." She grinned and stood, shifting around the house. She grabbed the book she'd been reading and settled back in her chair, but her interest just wasn't there. She washed the mugs from Sy's visit, dried them, and put them away. Fluffed the couch pillows, pulled together a load of laundry and put it in the machine, mopped the kitchen floor, and the hands on her antique clock had barely moved at all. She considered going for a run on her treadmill, but the thought of running in her basement just made her sad.

This must be what it feels like to be locked in a cell, she thought.

Beyond her windows, the day was so blue and the breeze warm and inviting. In another life she might have set out from her front door and gone down to Davis Bay to walk the promenade and talk to strangers along the way. People here on the Coast were known for being friendly, at least that was what she'd seen with her neighbors like Mrs. Whitcomb, though she'd likely chased them away with her lack of reciprocation.

Dammit, if that was what she wanted to do, then why not do it. Jude had thought it was safe, otherwise she wouldn't even have suggested it.

"All right. I get it." She set down the cloth she was going to dust with and looked at her sandaled feet. Sneakers would be better for a walk like this. Besides, sneakers were better for running in if she had to run away from anyone.

She changed into running shorts and a long t-shirt. She put on light canvas runners instead of her athletic shoes and grabbed her house keys, but started to sweat when she got to the front door. Her stomach flip-flopped and her palms were clammy.

Nooo. She could do this.

Quickly, before she could talk herself out of it, she flipped the locks, opened the door, and stepped outside, then pulled the door shut and locked it.

She felt dizzy. Her breath came in short, quick gasps. Well she wasn't going to get far trying to run like this. She'd asphyxiate herself.

Stepping down the porch stairs, she felt sweat running between her breasts. Walking down the front walk, she thought she might faint; but she made it to the street and stood there panting.

"Hello there, dear. Going for a walk?"

The disembodied female voice sent her stumbling back a pace, but then her neighbor Mrs. Whitcomb stuck her head up from pruning roses. The woman was in her sixties at least, with a net of fine wrinkles over her skin, but a youthful dewy look to her gaze.

"It's a beautiful day for it, and if I may say so, you don't get out enough. The Coast is a wonderful place to explore and be active with friends, you know. Why, I was saying to Robert the other night that you really need to make more friends. I was pleased to see that nice young man pop by to see you this morning." She smiled. "Very good looking, if I do say so myself. Now there was something I meant to tell you, but I can't recall what it was." She shook her head. "Honestly, this age thing addles the brain. If you don't mind, I'll pop over when I remember what it was. Would that be all right? I think it had something to do with the garden…"

Mrs. Whitcomb's effusive torrent of words almost took Cat's breath away.

"That would be fine," she managed to choke out. She waved goodbye and, fighting the desire to turn and run back into the house, she set off down the street at a breathless swinging stride.

The air seemed too close and the sun too hot on her head. She swallowed back the tremors she felt and kept going. She should have brought a hat, but if she went back to the house to get one, she knew she wouldn't come out. In the whole scheme of things, what did a little sunburn matter? She was out. She was proving that she was stronger than her fear. She was proving that Jude was wrong.

The street led down a slope to the two-lane highway and followed the grassy verge south along the edge of the highway for the one block to the Davis Bay promenade. Then she ducked through the infrequent traffic and she was back at the water, where Jude had brought her the day before. The tide wasn't as far out as it had been yesterday and the sandbars were all hidden by the waves. The rocky shore was scattered with driftwood and the ocean was crystal blue and calm in the bay, though farther out there were small waves. A tugboat chugged up the coast hauling a barge to the gravel port just a few miles north.

It was—beautiful. The gulls soared, an eagle cried in a pine treetop, and from down the beach in the neighborhood of Chapman Creek, an answering eagle cry floated back. Bald eagles, she'd learned, mated for life. They were good parents. Out on the water, a seal popped his head up and seemed to follow her as she continued walking. It felt wonderful to fill her lungs with open sea air and to move her limbs naturally instead of on a treadmill.

Her breathing came easier, though she jumped at male voices from a restaurant across the street. Other people walked the promenade and fishermen crowded the long pier that jutted into the water. On a weekday, it was a summertime crowd. Groups of school girls. Pairs of old women. Husbands and wives who looked retirement age. Even a courting boyfriend and girlfriendwho must be on holidays from work strolled the promenade. As each person or pair approached, she stiffened and was ready to run; but all she usually got was a smile and a nod. A few people said good morning, which she returned.

It was okay. She was okay and she'd been afraid for nothing. Her arms swung a little easier. Her stride lengthened. She could almost imagine running again. Letting her mind go in the sensations of her body as she ran down the pavement and turned up the street at the end of the promenade to wend her way home. Maybe she'd do that tomorrow.

Yes. Yes, she would.

She kept going to the park at Mission Point where Chapman's Creek ran into the sea. Tall cedar trees surrounded a lawn, an old orchard, picnic tables, and a public building used for art shows and meetings. She paused to step out on the jutting point of sandy beach. A large golden retriever was down among the rocks chasing the crows and sniffing amongst the seaweed. Cat watched him grab a ball from amongst the rocks and half toss it into the air before catching it again and trotting over beyond a patch of tall seagrass that blocked her view. The ball sailed out into the rocks again and the dog bounded after, came up with the ball, and came gamboling back, then must have ducked away from its owner.

"Harley! Here!" shouted a stern male voice.

The dog stopped his sidle away and pranced with the ball in its mouth.

"Harley!"

The dog pranced in place and then darted toward Cat's vantage. A dark figure gave chase beyond the rough stand of grass and Harley ran up to her and dropped the ball at her feet.

She raised her brow at the dog. "I don't think your owner wanted you to do that, fella."

"Here's the ball," she called and picked up the slobbery ball and tossed it across the grass toward the owner. Harley took after it at a bound. The ball appeared again in a long arc out toward the rocks and water. Harley chased after.

The dog's owner came around the edge of the grass. "Hey there! Thanks for the help."

Cat froze.

Tall. Broad shoulders with a weightlifter's build that he'd developed in prison gymnasiums, Kyle Redburn looked back at her.

"Sorry if Harley caused any problems. He's a tease with a ball."

Just like Kyle Redburn had said all women were teases and Cat Moore was worst of all, lording it over him. Well, he'd show her what was what and who was who.

She jolted back a step and blinked.

A tall, surfer-dude looking guy looked back at her. "Hey. You all right? You're white as a sheet."

Kyle Redburn or not, Cat turned and ran.

Didn't matter that she only had sneakers on and not her

athletic shoes. Didn't matter that she wasn't really dressed for it or that her chest was so tight she was running on empty.

Just get out of there. Just get home to safety.

She bolted down the park's dirt path, around the picnic area, and onto the concrete path along the promenade. Panicked, she shoved past walkers and lengthened her stride until she was halfway down the promenade and her head spun from lack of oxygen. She faltered and fell onto a park bench peering out at the water. Far down the beach back the way she'd come, a yellow dog frolicked on the spit of beach and rock spilling out into the water.

It hadn't been Kyle Redburn.

That was pretty clear, given she'd seen the surfer dude a moment later. Maybe her subconscious was expecting Kyle given she'd thought she'd seen him at the grocery store.

Or maybe being housebound all this time had finally driven her crazy. Or maybe, as Kyle Redburn had said as he beat her, she'd been a crazy bitch all along. He'd beaten and humiliated her and left her for dead. The only thing he hadn't done was rape her.

She gulped air and sat up straighter. Surely, she wasn't crazy. She wasn't doing weird things or seeing anything else. But then, who was she to judge? She could even doubt that there had been a cougar in her yard, except that Sy Foster had come and the cat had proved real enough for him to rescue the animal.

Thoughts of the cougar and Sy left her calmer. She pushed to standing and headed for home, uncertain whether she'd ever step out of the house again. But if she didn't, she was simply giving into her fear and proving that she was, indeed, a little off her rocker. The government and victim services had offered her counseling after the beating incident, but she'd viewed accepting it as a sign of weakness that would put a black mark on her employee record. No one in the Corrections Branch wanted to employ a weak link. And her background as a victim would make every decision she made—and every recommendation to the court—fodder for defense counsels. She'd spend her life on the witness stand defending herself.

No, she was fine all by herself.

Unless she wasn't.

She was sweating as she climbed the hill to her house. From behind her, a small blue car chugged past and then pulled into the side of the road. For a moment she thought it was Jude come to make up, but no one got out. Probably just someone stopping to use their smart phone. There were more people stopping since the government put heavy fines on distracted driving.

She turned down her street and sped up. Ahead, the house seemed to gleam in the sunlight. There was safety. There she could breathe without her chest feeling like it would burst. There she wouldn't have to look over her shoulder all the time.

She half-jogged the last fifty feet and down her walkway, then fumbled her keys out of her pocket and into the lock.

The rumble of a car engine made her glance over her shoulder. The same small blue car, she was sure of it. It slowed as it passed her, the driver's side window scrolling down.

Kyle Redburn looked back at her and grinned.

She opened her door and fell in.

8

———————

S y turned off the highway up the street toward Cat's house feeling rather proud of himself. If Mohammed wouldn't come to the mountain, he'd take the mountain to Mohammed. Or at least he'd take dinner. The truck cab smelled deliciously of the ribs and potato salad he'd ordered from *Rack o' Ribs,* the Sunshine Coast's premier rib institution, and picked up a few minutes ago. He could feel the heat escaping the foil-wrapped package. The potato salad, on the other hand, was packed on ice to keep it fresh. On the floor was a bottle of red wine and a six pack of locally brewed craft beer.

A veritable feast, if not the restaurant meal he'd envisioned. In some ways this might be a better option. It would allow Cat to stay in comfortable surroundings while they got to know each other. It was becoming pretty clear that Cat wasn't too comfortable leaving her house for some reason—other than her rather exceptional venture out to the refuge.

Hopefully she'd be surprised—in a good way. He didn't fancy eating all those ribs and all that salad himself.

In front of the house, he pulled the truck in, the tires

crunching in the gravel verge of the road. He gathered his packages and climbed out, then looked at the house.

Unlike earlier, the front curtains were closed. So were the curtains in the other street facing rooms. Odd. But then sometimes people closed curtains to stop the sun from streaming in and heating the house. Except this was the northeast side of the house.

Concerned, he headed down the walk to the door and up onto the porch. Juggling the food, he managed to knock.

There was no sound from inside.

He knocked again.

Still nothing. Maybe Cat was outside on the porch and didn't hear him. After all, he wasn't exactly expected.

He left the wrapped food and drink on the porch, silently warned off the murder of crows in the trees, and went down along the side of the house to peer up at the porch. Not there and the folding glass doors were firmly shut, yet for some reason he was pretty sure that Cat was there. It was as if he could feel her gaze on him, sense her heartbeat near.

Praying no one called the police on him as a cat burglar, he climbed the rear stairs to the patio. More curtains pulled across the view and Cat had seemed to love that view. In fact, it seemed to feed her when everything else about her said she was locked away.

Except for that brief moment when she'd touched his hand yesterday. He could still feel that light touch and the softness of her skin under her lips from when he'd kissed her cheek.

He rapped on the folding glass doors. "Cat? It's me, Sy. Are you okay?"

Still nothing. Concern bloomed to worry. Had something happened to her?

"Cat, please. Just let me know that you're okay."

Was that a stirring he heard in the house? Perhaps the pad of bare feet on hardwood? Did the curtain over the door twitch at the edge?

"Cat. Talk to me! If you don't, I'll have no choice but to call the police—or break down the door myself!" He was surprised to realize that he meant it.

"Don't!" The single word came muffled through the glass.

"Cat! Are you okay?" He shifted to where he'd seen the curtain twitch. "Come on, Cat. Open the curtain and let me see you."

"I—I hardly know you. Why are you here?" The voice was hoarse, as if she'd been crying.

Good question. "I brought dinner. You said you didn't go out, so I thought we could eat in and get to know each other. I'd really like to get to know you, Cat."

And he meant it, unlike all those centuries ago when he simply took anything that was of a passing interest, including women— regardless of what his wife, the women, or the women's husbands felt. For a moment he mourned for those women of so long ago.

The curtain twitched and parted to expose a single huge misty brown eye. "You don't want to know me. Not anymore."

He shook his head. "I'm afraid that ship has sailed, Cat. I've met you, and I do."

She blinked back a tear. "I'm sorry, Sy. I c-c-can't. I don't even think I can open the door."

"What is it? What's happened?" He reached toward her, but was stopped by the glass. Damn, he wanted to take her in his arms and soothe whatever was causing her so much pain.

She twisted away from the small opening in the curtain and he thought he'd lost her. "Cat, no! Talk to me. Tell me what's wrong."

The curtain tugged a little farther open. Her hair was a tangled blonde cap and her face was pale, with bright peaks on her cheekbones as if she was fevered. She wore running shorts on her slim thighs and a loose white t-shirt that showed signs of sweat.

"I'm what's wrong. I've been scared so long that I've locked myself away and now I—I think I'm seeing things."

The locking herself away wasn't a surprise although he hadn't realized how bad her condition was. But seeing things? From what he'd seen of Cat Moore, she was a realistic person. "What are you seeing, Cat?"

"The man who tried to kill me."

"What?" It felt like the world shrink-wrapped in around him and all that mattered was the woman on the other side of the window.

"Cat, please. I'll help you. All you have to do is tell me what happened. If you're in danger, we need to call the police and report it." He tried to meet her gaze, but she kept her eyes downturned.

Zeus above, he needed her to let him in. "Cat, you listen to me. If you saw something, I believe you. I haven't known you very long, but you strike me as a reliable sort of person. You wouldn't make this kind of thing up."

She shook her head. "I don't know anymore." She looked up at him like a broken-winged owl. "What if I don't know what's real anymore?"

"Then..." He ran his hands back through his hair. "Then we'll figure it out together. We'll get you help if you need it. If it's true, I'll keep you safe."

She sniffed and shook her head. "It's dangerous for you to be involved, Sy. This man has seriously hurt people beyond me."

But it was her he was concerned about.

"Just let me in and we'll decide what to do."

Finally, she looked up at him and met his gaze.

"Okay? You're not in this alone, Cat. I'm here, too. Now open the door and let me in so that we can talk."

She barely nodded and he held his breath, but she stepped forward and clicked open the lock on the folding doors.

He let out a breath as he quickly slid the door open far enough that he could slip inside. Then he closed and locked the door behind him. If she was that scared, he wasn't going to demand that the door remain open. He turned to her.

She drooped where she stood and he stepped up to her, hesitated, and then gently pulled her into his chest. She stiffened, but he kept his grip loose. Gradually she relaxed to sag against him, her head resting just under his chin. Slowly, so as not to startle her, he lifted his left hand and cupped her head. His right hand lightly held the small of her back.

"I'm here for you, Cat. No matter what's happening, I am."

The strange thing was, after all the millennia of his selfish life, this time he meant it.

Cat was cold, so cold, and Sy's warm embrace felt like the first time in her life she'd ever been warm. Around them her house was filled with shadows, just like her head. Too many shadows that might hide dangers, but that she could hide in herself; and yet with Sy's muscled arms around her and inhaling his clean male scent of soap and water, they didn't seem quite so dark, the danger not quite so great.

After seeing the blue car and its driver, she'd been frozen in the entryway. When she'd come to herself fifteen minutes later, she'd plunged through the house, locking doors and windows and pulling curtains closed, so the house felt stuffy and too warm. Then she'd come into the great room by the kitchen where she could see the front and rear of the house and the stairs to the lower floor. She'd spent the rest of the day guarding them, startling at every creak and groan of the house and every street sound.

When Sy had knocked on the door, she'd almost screamed. Instead she'd quietly snuck into the kitchen and armed herself with a butcher knife from her knife block. This time—this time she'd defend herself. Kyle Redburn wasn't getting away unscathed this time.

But it hadn't been Kyle. It had been Sy and when she'd heard his voice she'd forced herself to set the knife down and to listen to him. Part of her had wanted to run into the bathroom and slam and lock the door. Instead a better part of her had prevailed and she had twitched the curtain open.

With his arms around her, she was glad she had. She pressed into his chest, amazed at the strength and yet gentleness she felt in his arms and the amazing safety she felt.

His palm stroked her hair and she would have purred had she been a feline. Instead she pulled away because she was stronger than this. She had to be. She swiped at her eyes.

"I'm sorry. I'm really not a hysterical female." The trouble was, she really didn't have an excuse for feeling the way she did, other than Kyle Redburn, and that was ancient history.

Sy caught her shoulders. "You don't strike me as particularly hysterical. A hysterical woman wouldn't have been able to help with the cougar like you did and I doubt that a hysterical woman would have persevered and cleaned out the bat shed." He tipped his head down at her. "You listening to what I said?"

"Sure. But you barely know me. You didn't know me— before. I—I wasn't like this then."

He ran his hands up and down her arms. "If that's the case, you must have been pretty amazing before, because you seem pretty terrific now, too."

The soft words brought her head up and she met his gaze. He meant what he said, but he had nothing to base his comment on.

"Listen, why don't we sit down and you can tell me what happened before and what happened today that scared you so badly."

He urged her toward the couch and she finally settled into the deep cushions and cream fabric. Sy sat across from her in a sky-blue chair, and sunlight through the spaces between the curtains placed dust mote bars through the air.

"So?" he asked, his face in shadows.

She stopped herself from wringing her hands and leaned back and closed her eyes. "It was two years ago. I worked at the Langley Probation Office. I was a probation officer and did sentencing reports for the court. There was a man who had been on my caseload. He was always trying to flirt, but I never responded. You never do with these guys because they can fixate on you. Anyway, he got picked up for a couple of assaults on women committed during break and enters. He was out on bail awaiting sentencing and I was ordered to complete a presentence report. I did, and the report was submitted to the prosecutor, to defense counsel, and to the judge. Given the man's lengthy history and poor performance on probation, I recommended a significant jail sentence."

It felt so familiar dropping into her Probation Officer persona, but now the story got harder. She cleared her throat and forced herself to go on even though a cold sweat had formed on her body and her breath was coming in short little gasps again.

"Of course, defense counsel provided the report to his client. I guess Kyle was furious. I was working late one day with another female officer. We always tried to work in pairs. She wanted to head home and I still had a few things to do and nothing had ever happened, so I said it was okay for her to head home. When I finally left an hour later, Kyle Redburn was waiting for me in the parking lot."

She remembered his figure as he stepped out from behind the garbage bin toward her. She remembered the furious look on his face, his fist driving toward her face and then his silhouette against the sky above her, the pavement under her, his boots and fists slamming into her. His laughter.

"He beat me until I was almost dead. I would have been if a street person hadn't come by and called the police. Kyle Redburn was long gone by the time the police and paramedics came, and I spent a month in hospital and six months off work. I tried to go back, but I froze every time a client walked into my office. They tried to find me another job, but by then I could barely go out of the house. Finally, they put me on a disability pension and here I am."

She clutched her hands between her knees and looked at him. "I've been a shut-in since it happened. I never went out in Langley; I was too afraid. So I sold there and bought here thinking it would allow me to start over, but I brought the fear with me. My friend Jude said that I had to start getting out or I was never going to have a life again. I thought she was wrong and we had a horrible fight and that was when I went up to the refuge to prove she was wrong." She shook her head. Sy's face remained impassive and ready, like a sponge soaking it all in.

"The day before yesterday Jude tried to get me out. We went to the beach and then to the grocery store, but I stayed in the car at the store. While I was waiting, I was sure that I spotted Kyle Redburn and he saw me, too. Then today I decided to go down to the beach on foot, on my own, to prove to myself that I could have a life. I went down there and there was this guy with a dog. I couldn't see him well at first because of some tall grass, but then he stepped around the grass and I was as certain as I am that you are you, that it was Kyle Redburn. Then I blinked and it was a blond guy. I turned and ran. I ran almost all the way home and just as I got to my street…" She swallowed and closed her eyes and told him about the car that seemed to have followed her and how it had driven past and Kyle Redburn had stared out at her and smiled.

She shivered and the tremors wouldn't stop.

Sy shifted to sit beside her and put his arm around her shoulders.

"No wonder you were terrified," he said as if he was talking to himself. He leaned back and pulled her back into the crook of his shoulder. "And you weren't sure you should call police because you weren't sure you'd really seen him. But how come he wasn't arrested before now?"

"He disappeared after he beat me, and even though there's a warrant, he hasn't been seen since. He's clearly been keeping a low profile."

"So why come after you now, two years later?" he asked.

"I have no idea." But it was a really good question. She sat up, considering. "To finish the job is what I've been thinking, but that doesn't necessarily make sense. Maybe—maybe he wants something else." For the life of her she couldn't think what.

Finally, she shook her head, drew in a deep breath, and met Sy's gaze. "I don't know what he could want or even if it was really him, but you I do know. Thank you for coming this afternoon. What brought you here, anyway?"

Sy frowned and suddenly his face cleared and he laughed. He sprang up from the couch. "Hold that thought. I'll be right back."

He headed off to the front of the house and out the front door, then returned carrying bags and parcels he retrieved from the front porch. He held them up, triumphant. "Dinner, m'lady!"

The scent of barbeque preceded him into the room and he went into her kitchen and turned the oven on. He put the metal tray he carried in the oven and the large brown bag into the fridge. From a small brown bag he produced a bottle of red wine. He held it up, looking a question at her. "Now or with dinner?"

She didn't know what to say, mostly because she was a little distracted at how he seemed to belong in her kitchen. That and the athletic way he moved. She liked that about him. In fact, she liked *him,* and that wasn't just because he was virtually the first male she had come to know since her self-imposed exile from the human race.

Because it had been self-imposed. Friends from the office

had tried to be there for her and she'd shut them out because she was embarrassed. They'd ceased trying probably because she was a reminder of the chink in their armor. No probation officer was armed in this jurisdiction. They had to trust to static measures of protection like secure parking. The Corrections Branch had upgraded all their security after her beating, but it was only a matter of time before another Kyle Redburn did his thing.

"How about now?" she said. "A nice red wine would taste good and probably taste good with that barbeque. What is it, by the way?"

He grinned at her before eyeing her cupboards and somehow knew exactly where she kept her wine glasses. He pulled out two red wine glasses, opened the bottle, and poured. "What is for dinner is a delicious concoction made by a local barbeque virtuoso, who I discovered a few years ago. The specifics of the meal you will have to wait and see."

He handed her a glass and she sipped.

"Mm. Good." She grabbed the bottle and looked. "Italian, no less. I thought everyone was into Australian or South American."

"That was last year. This is from close to the old country. I discovered it a few years back, too. Luckily they keep producing good wine and no one seems to be the wiser. Let the hordes drink Australian." He led her back to the couch and they settled together.

"Do you mind?" He said, setting his wine down and going to the heavy curtains that blocked the view.

Kyle Redburn could be outside the window. He could be in the yard. He could be watching. She took a deep breath and nodded. "This wine will be better with a view."

"So will the meal," Sy said and used the draw cord to smoothly pull the curtains open, revealing the amber-streaked sky of sunset. There was going to be a doozy of a show tonight. "Shall I open the door?" he asked casually.

Before she could protest, he unlocked and pushed open the sliding glass doors. A gust of sweet evening air flooded in carrying the scent of gardens, cut lawns, and the ocean. The cool, fresh air was a balm on her skin and in her lungs. She closed her eyes and listened to the distant hum of the ocean and felt the couch cushions shift under her as Sy returned to his seat.

When she opened her eyes, she found him watching her.

"I love the scent of the ocean and the creamy feel of the air. I feel like I get a facial every time I step out the door."

Sy nodded. "It's pretty good air. Not that I'd ever imagine you getting a facial."

"Thanks." She could take a compliment. "I'm not getting any younger, you know. But then I guess no one is."

A sad expression crossed his face, but then he reached across and gently touched her cheek. "In my mind you will always be this age." Then he seemed to come to himself and he pulled his hand back as if burned. "Sorry."

He sprang up again as if he was nervous. "Let me check on dinner."

He left her for the kitchen and Cat sat sipping her very good wine filled with licorice, fruit, and tannins and watched Sy as he shifted from oven to fridge and back again. He hauled down a large platter that she had on display and a large bowl that she usually used for mashed potatoes and then was busy arranging his secret deliciousness before turning to reveal dinner.

Long racks of pork and beef ribs lay slathered in bubbling barbecue sauce.

Cat looked from the delicious feast to Sy. "I think I might kiss you. Do you know I can't recall the last time I ate and I didn't think I was hungry. I thought I should force to myself to eat something healthy so I was going to have a salad."

She shook her head as Sy whisked the brown paper bag out of the fridge and produced two quart-sized containers of salad—one potato and the other Greek.

Her mouth watered. "Hold on."

She pulled plates from the cupboard and serving spoons and knives and forks from a drawer. Then she found a handful of large paper napkins. She drove the serving spoons into the salads and looked at him expectantly.

"You have a choice. We can be civilized and eat at the table, or we can be wild and crazy and have a picnic right here on the floor." She nodded at the carpet between the couch and the open glass doors.

Sy eyed the table and then the floor. Then he shrugged. "I guess I'm in for wild and crazy..."

With a nod, she put the knives, forks, and napkins on the floor where she and Sy could sit with their backs to the couch and watch the sunset. She might not be able to go out for a picnic, but she could imagine the experience. It was nice of Sy to go along with her craziness.

She caught up to Sy as he stacked too many ribs on her plate. She confiscated said plate and then proceeded to pile on the salad. "God help me, I think I've lost my mind, but it all looks and smells so good."

She sank cross-legged to the floor and set the plate on the cross of her legs. Sy settled beside her, legs outstretched, and balanced his plate there. He picked up his wine glass and nodded her to hers.

He clinked her glass.

"What are we toasting?" Cat asked.

"Meetings. Dinners. Sunsets. Does it matter?" His gaze was deep and clouded as the wine, but his lips formed a strong, curved line. He lifted his glass to her. "To injured cougars and healing."

He sipped his wine and leaned back against the couch to set down his glass and begin on his food.

"Cougars and healing," Cat echoed and followed his example.

The meat was every bit as good as it smelled. Fall-off-the-bone tender meat, swathed in sweet and spicy sauce that quickly covered her fingers and lips. It didn't matter and quickly the heaped plate she never thought she could finish was filled with nothing but licked-clean bones. She forked the last of her mustard and celery seed flavored mayo and potato salad into her mouth and chewed with relish, then sipped her wine.

The sky was tinged apricot with ruby streamers as the sun fell farther over the rim of the world. Above, the blue sky was washing out before the tidal inflow of nighttime. The air cooled. The distant sound of traffic slowed. The great comforting lull of the ocean washed through her, or maybe it was a replete stomach, a good glass of wine and the very nice—no, the very good-looking man beside her.

She sipped her wine and realized the glass had been refilled. She felt—relaxed. More relaxed than she'd felt any time over the past two years. It was as if she and Sy inhabited a precious, private space between daytime and nighttime—a place Kyle Redburn could never go.

Savoring the wine, she peered out into the evening, afraid to break the spell.

"You know, I was pretty pleased that you made the trek to the refuge and then stayed," Sy said quietly as if he too sensed the tremulous moment they inhabited together.

She glanced over and found him watching her again. He'd set their plates aside and had crossed his long legs. They were good legs. His Bermuda shorts exposed his calves and thighs, tanned and strongly muscled as if from long years of labor or a severe fitness regimen. His entire body was long and lean like an athlete's. He likely didn't have much use for people who allowed themselves to go to seed.

His gaze on her was watchful, but she couldn't look away and it was as if a power current that had been pulsing quietly suddenly arced through the air. He set his wine glass down and leaned over to her to catch her chin in his fingers. Then, gently, he leaned in for a kiss.

Soft. Exploratory. His lips hard and yet gentle as he tasted her mouth.

The feel of his mouth on hers left her momentarily breathless, yet wanting more. She found herself leaning into him, but then he leaned back against the couch, stared out at the water and nodded.

"What? What is the nod for?"

"Your lips tasted just like I expected," he said without even looking at her.

"And what's that?" she asked dryly.

"Barbeque. The best damn barbeque on the coast. And you, of course. Lotus flower, I think."

"Right. And you've eaten a lot of lotus flower, have you?"

He leaned in close. "I have a feeling that I could forget myself in you."

She wanted to laugh at the sweetness that surely no one could truly mean, but his hand came up to tenderly cup the back of her head. This time he didn't need to draw her in. She leaned into him, raising her mouth to his.

Magic.

It was a slow, lingering kiss of exploration. Lips grazed over her mouth as she did the same to him, tentative, testing, and finding she liked the taste of him, the feel of his mouth next to hers, the scent of his breath mingling with hers: barbeque and maleness.

Surprising herself, she rose to her knees and turned toward him.

His hands slid down to her shoulders and arms and this time it was she who leaned into him, her lips exploring the edge of his mouth. His hands steadied her as his lips opened to meet her and he drank her in. Hard lips, exploring tongue that danced in her mouth.

Heat flared through her and she trembled. Sy pulled her into his chest, her legs across his lap. He held her to him.

"This is very strange," he murmured into her hair. "I never in my life expected to feel like this." He chuckled, a good rumbling sound in his chest. "The gods are jokesters."

"Gods?" she asked, looking up at him.

"A figure of speech." His arms tightened around her.

For the first time in what seemed like a lifetime, she felt safe. She nodded into his chest. "If it's any consolation, I never expected this, either. Anyone ever tell you you're a good kisser?"

"Nope." He arched a brow at her. "What, in particular, is it that I do well?"

Still in his lap, she sat up to face him. "Well… there's the way you let your lips graze mine."

"Like this?" He lowered his head to her and his lips trailed small kisses across her mouth, her jaw, and into her hairline. His touch and his warm breath on her skin stoked a fire she didn't remember having. She arched her neck to one side to allow him access and his mouth trailed up to her ear where he lightly nibbled her lobe. Sparks flashed behind her eyelids and she groaned.

"Yes. That's one of the things about your kissing." It came out a little ragged.

He chuckled, and his incendiary lips trailed down her neck, spreading the fire that was slowly growing inside her. It was as if she'd been frozen for a thousand years and suddenly the sunlight had warmed the ice. She ran her fingers through his hair and inhaled sharply as his lips found the edge of her sleeveless t-shirt.

Sy lifted his head to her in question.

"It's okay. I—I want this. I—I feel like I've been hobbling around wounded like that cougar for too long. I want to heal. I want to be a whole woman again."

Still he hesitated, his gaze dark and wary.

She shook her head, frustrated with herself. "I'm not saying this right. I want you, Sy Foster."

Before she lost her nerve, she released his head and tugged her t-shirt up over her head, then tossed it aside. It was madness doing this when she hardly knew this man, but…

She was committing to this and it was exhilarating.

And terrifying.

9

———————

The sunset had faded, turning the horizon to burning hues of dark vermillion and amber and staining the creamy flesh before him to dusty rose. A fresh breeze blew through the patio's open doors carrying the sound of the ocean and the scent of someone's rose garden. Or perhaps that was Cat Moore's own scent. It filled his senses and left him wanting more.

She was trim and pale, her skin almost translucent so that faint traceries of veins made her appear even more delicate than her slim limbs and fine bones suggested. And yet she was strong. Strong enough to survive what had happened to her and to want to establish a new life. Strong enough to expose herself to him as a potential lover after all that she had been through.

The question was whether she truly felt something for him or whether this was simply something therapeutic for her. Because he wasn't kidding when he said he felt something for her.

Cat Moore was special in a way that no woman before had ever been. Not even Merope, his long dead wife, had inspired him like this. Merope he had cared for only as long as she did as he bid her, and even then, after she had done as he had bid and *not* completed the ceremonies and sacrifices that should have been completed at his death, he reached out to her from hell to punish her for her omission. He had been cruel and obsessed with meeting only his own needs. He had stolen and overthrown and murdered. Even after millennia of rolling a stone up a hill, had he absolved himself of those past crimes?

He didn't think so, and yet this pale-skinned beauty was offering herself to him.

He groaned and closed his eyes, sinking back against the couch and loosening his hold on Cat. It felt like losing a part of himself.

"Sy?" His name trembled in the air.

He opened his eyes to look at her, so lovely and delicate. Just looking at her, his body responded, but…

"Are you sure this is a good idea? You had a horrible scare today." And that was likely all this was for her, an attempt to make herself feel alive after being afraid for her life.

"Are you suggesting that is why I'm sitting in your lap half naked?"

She suddenly scrambled up and strode across to her shirt, tugged it on. She turned to face him, her expression clear even in the failing light. Cat Moore was not happy and frankly the fire in her gaze was even more of a turn-on.

He hauled himself up to standing, hoping his feelings weren't too obvious in his loose shorts.

"Cat, no. I just don't want this to be about the wrong things. I want you to be sure. I don't want to hurt you."

She glared up at him. "When is anyone sure? Anyone can hurt anyone, anytime. Life's a crapshoot, Sy Foster. You either live your life or you might as well curl up and die. That's what I was doing and I don't want to do it anymore."

Her chest rose and fell rapidly. The vein in her jaw pulsed. She looked up at him so ferociously he wasn't quite sure what to say.

"So what *do* you want?" he finally asked softly.

Her gaze steadied on him, but her eyes narrowed. "You."

In two strides she crossed to him and placed her arms around his neck. His hands came up around her back and he hauled her into him and buried his face in her hair. Gods in Olympus, he was going to end up back in Hades again, pushing that boulder up that hill for another millennia, but he wanted this woman and he wanted her now.

He swept her into his arms in a second and lifted her off her feet. "Where?" as he swung around with her in his arms. He banged his shin on the edge of a table, stumbled, and almost tripped over the dishes on the floor.

"Down the hall." Her voice was ragged and she reached for him, pulled his mouth down to hers, and kissed him deeply so he staggered against the wall.

"First door to the right," she breathed into his mouth as she trailed inflamed kisses down neck and chest.

Sy stumbled into her bedroom doorframe. With the closed curtains the room was dark. He waited for his eyes to adjust and saw a king-sized bed covered in a pristine white quilt. A heap of multicolored pillows sat at the head of the bed, though the darkness had stolen their colors away. A sliding barn door painted white presumably hid a closet and ensuite. An overstuffed white armchair stood in the corner by the curtained window. Books and a digital alarm rested on one bedside table.

The sultry-sweet scent of frankincense wafted from somewhere in the room. He recognized it from his past life when it had been a favorite of his. Such a scent, the precious product of a rare tree in what today was the country of Oman, he had had in his chambers long ago. He thought it had been lost in antiquity because he had not smelled it since his release from Hades all those centuries after his death. And yet here it was.

He inhaled deeply and peered down at the woman in his arms. Lightly she kissed his chest, her fingers tugged down the round neck of his t-shirt. There were so many contradictions in

Cat Moore. On the one hand she was terrified and fragile and on the other she was as strong as anyone he knew and not afraid to be the aggressor sexually. It was refreshing. It was actually sexy as hell. Each time he learned about one of Cat Moore's many facets he found himself more attracted to her. He wasn't sure it was a good thing, but he was prepared to go with it—for now.

At the bed he laid her down and she rolled onto her side to face him. He stretched out beside her fully clothed. This—this was a time for tenderness and exploration, like cherishing the discovery of a new lake's shoreline and learning the flora and fauna that dwelt there. Do no harm. Leave nothing behind that was not there before.

No hurt, at least.

He leaned in to kiss her and rolled her onto her back. Against the snowy white of the coverlet, her creamy skin was tanned and smooth. He inhaled her scent of roses, gently held her face in his hands, and kissed her firmly. Her lips parted and her arms came up around him as he drank her in like heady wine. Softness and warmth and desire. Wine and barbeque and woman.

His hands sleeked down her shoulders to her sides and upward to cup her breasts, still hidden in her bra and t-shirt.

"Mm," she hummed, smiled into their kiss, and arched her back slightly into his hands.

His body responded as he lightly ran his palms over her rock-hard nipples. After all this time of abstention, he was going to do this. He pulled her up off the bed and tugged her t-shirt up and over her head. Tossed it aside as she dragged his shirt up his back. He shucked it off and they stared at each other in the dark.

Cat's gaze fell away to her hands in her lap. "It's been a long time since I've been with a man… I hope it's not disappointing."

He chuckled. "About the farthest thing from it. You, Cat Moore, are beautiful. I wonder why you don't know it?"

She raised her gaze to him then. "I have these scars." She

lightly touched her temple where he'd noticed a small scar arch across her brow. Her hand fluttered away and down to her side.

He bent and lightly kissed her lips. "And you are the woman I am with, scars and all. Scars are simply signs of life. Signs of healing we've done. They are history written in flesh."

He trailed kisses down her neck to her bra strap and easily slipped it out of his way off her shoulder. Then he trailed his hot breath lower, down to the lace that cupped her breasts. He didn't touch, simply breathed on them and felt her tense and give the faintest of moans.

"I think we should get rid of this, don't you?" Without waiting for an answer, he flicked open the rear closure and the bra slid loosely down her shoulders. He tugged it off and tossed it after her shirt.

Perfect small breasts as he'd imagined. Nipples almost as pale as her skin. He ran his fingers lightly over her shoulders and down to her breasts, stroking the tender undersides before using his thumb and forefinger to take a nipple and squeeze.

Cat moaned and her back arched. He leaned down to capture her other nipple in his mouth and tongued it so her arms came up and held his head as if she could not get enough. She scrambled to her knees and he found the closure of her shorts and swiftly shoved them down over her trim hips. She sidled out of them and then swung a leg over his lap. At the descent of her warmth, his hard length throbbed in his shorts. He held her to him and she rubbed herself against his length. Her smaller hands explored across his chest, her neat nails teasing his nipple nubbins. He groaned.

Damn shorts. He could rip her underwear off her and plunge inside her if he didn't still have them on.

He eased Cat back on the bed, his head full of her scent, of glimpses of her gaze, darkened by the night. Of her blonde hair trailing silk over his skin, then fanning around her face on the bed. He stood up and swiftly removed the rest of his clothing.

Her gaze lingered over his length. She sat up and reached for his hand, then tugged him closer to the bed, her hands sliding coolly to his ass as she stroked him and ran her breath and tongue tip teasingly over him.

When she took him in her mouth, he thought he might come then and there—it had been that long. He concentrated on the power it took to get that infernal boulder up the hill as her mouth worked over him and his balls tightened. Tightened further.

"Stop now or you're going to finish this too early," he groaned and held her head away. He eased her back onto her back. "My turn."

He kissed her deeply, then ran his kisses down to her breasts to pause there for a time until she squirmed under him and panted with need.

His left hand stroked her side and down to her flat belly. It rippled under his touch as he stroked lower, keeping her cursed silken panties between their flesh. She groaned and pressed up into his palm, thrusting at him with want.

"Not yet, my sweet," he smiled into her belly and slid lower down her body. Snagging the top edge with his fingers, her panties slid easily off her hips to expose a small bush of pale blonde curls. He trailed kisses over her belly and teased her nipples with his right hand as he kissed her inner thighs and then took her in his mouth.

She froze under him and then his tongue released her with a cry. She spread her legs wider for him and he licked her, feeling her tremble under him and the trembling grow. And grow.

She spasmed under him again and again and he smiled to himself as he lifted above her.

"Now?" she panted, through her bliss. "More?"

"Greedy." He tickled her side and she shrieked as she threw her legs around his waist and pulled herself upright to face him.

"Greedy, yes!" She hissed up at him, her gaze gleaming as if she would take him right now.

"A condom," he said and pulled one from his wallet. He had learned long ago to keep with the times. She took it from him and smoothly rolled it on, then smiled shyly up at him as she positioned herself over his length.

She shifted her hips and he entered her, her gasp one of delight.

He caught her hips and held her as he drove himself inside.

Her head fell back and she cried out softly, then began to move, driving into him and using her linked legs around his back to bring him ever deeper inside.

Through the barrier of the condom, he felt her slick insides. Felt her walls give way as she allowed him entry to the deepest heart of her. And still it wasn't enough. He wanted more. By the urgency of her thrusting hips, so did she. Holding her close so their union remained intact, he leaned her back onto the coverlet and rose above her, plunging ever deeper. She thrust her hips up to meet him, but it wasn't enough. Never enough with Cat Moore.

Her short, sharp cries urged him on and for a moment the long centuries of regret fell away and there was only now. This moment and the pale-skinned woman who opened her eyes. In the darkness their gazes met, joined, and became one. One single being and Sy fell into Cat's gaze.

The way his hard body shifted over hers, the way the hard length of him held her to the bed and left her wanting more with each plunge, it was if this wasn't just the first time with Sy, it was the first time ever! Her body melted around him, reformed, and became a new woman. A woman with crazy need for the man above her. She grabbed his ass and held on. Wrapped her legs tighter, but he grabbed her knees and shifted her position so that he found new depths inside her to fill.

She kissed his face, his shoulders, the arms braced to either side of her head. Wanted to touch-kiss-love every masculine inch of this man. Wanted this moment to never end.

This was a man who was all male. He attracted something atavistic in her. She might have always considered herself a liberated woman, but that was gone now. She was something older. Earth goddess? Demeter? Athena? No, Artemis, who the Romans called Diana. The huntress. That was how she felt. She had her power back with this man and what she wanted now was him.

Waves of pleasure washed over her and made fear impossible. Made thoughts impossible, as well. Just the sensations that radiated out from her core, stealing her strength, erasing the years of tension. She was melting. A pool. And yet the explosion built within her. The tight pleasure of her core tightened further, further, like a band pulled to breaking.

Sy went to his knees and raised his body above her. He pulled her farther onto him. "I want you to come," he said as he slowed the rhythm to a pleasurable slide that made her want to scream, want to demand his plunge deep within her. When she thrust her hips, he tut-tutted.

"Slow down, little one. Enjoy." His hands were busy. One holding her steady as he kept up his slow slide in and out. The other slid up her exposed belly to fondle her breasts, squeeze her nipples so she thought she might die for the pleasure it wrought. She turned her face sideways, embarrassed by the wanton need that must fill her face. She felt exposed and yet—with Sy it was safe.

His hands sleeked down her sides and one began to fondle her dampness, found her spot, and tweaked it.

The darkness exploded in lightning flashes that bolted through her flesh, her head. Her body shuddered, shuddered again. Wouldn't stop shuddering as Sy picked up rhythm. As he held her hips and drove into her wetness. The room filled with the sounds of their meeting, their cries, their union.

Sy tensed above her and drove inside her one more time. Drove deeper than before and she was holding on tight to the bedding, to his hands that held her hips as he groaned and pulsed inside her as her shudders roared through her and she couldn't breathe, couldn't see, could barely hear over the roar of her heartbeat, the blood in her ears. And then Sy collapsed forward on his elbows, his warm breath on her face as he cupped her cheek with his palm. His kiss lingered on her lips before he pulled back and grinned. His teeth were white in the dimness.

"Now that…that was something." He trailed kisses down her cheek and neck to her breast and suckled there a moment. Her insides trembled and convulsed still around him.

"Wow!" She whispered, her fingers in his hair as she luxuriated in the pleasure his touch evoked. "I don't think it's ever been like that." She was still coming, thought the tremors might never end and how would she ever think with this much pleasure rattling her brains. But maybe that was a good thing.

Sy pulled out and quickly went to the bathroom, then returned sans condom and stretched beside her. His callused palms stroked her sides so she could almost purr as she snuggled into the crook of his shoulder.

His breath had slowed, though she could still feel his roaring pulse. He leaned down and kissed her forehead as his arm curled her in to his chest. His tanned skin looked dark against her white bedspread.

"We might have to keep doing this until we get it right," he said with a small shake of his head.

Cat swallowed back the need to start right now. "You're suggesting that there was something wrong with that?"

Sy reached over and gently tweaked a nipple. "There had to be. Nothing is ever exactly right the first time."

"Really?" She reached down to stroke his flaccid length and

felt him grow hard in her hand. "Then I guess we should get on that right away. Practice makes perfect and all that."

Sy batted her hand away. "You are a wicked woman." But his hands smoothed down her sides and then picked her up to straddle him.

And so began another, more languorous bout of lovemaking. Cat impaled herself on him and began to slowly, ever so slowly move, rising and falling along his length.

It was dark and the house was silent when Cat woke from a brief nap between their lovemaking. The room was dark, only the barest of light creeping around the edge of the bedroom curtains. The moon must be up.

Sy sprawled beside her, his arm draped comfortingly warm over her waist, his handsome face turned toward her. Even asleep and in the darkness, she could see the strength of him. Something—honest physical work—had etched itself on his features as well as in the muscles of his shoulders and thighs and the calluses of his hands. His ultimate male musk made her legs weak and she almost woke him up again, the need for him throbbed so badly in her core.

If she stayed here, she'd do exactly that, so she eased out from under his arm and rolled to sitting on the edge of the bed. The room smelled of their sex and the floor was strewn with their discarded clothes. She had to smile.

Strong fingers caught her arm.

"Come back to bed," Sy's sleepy voice purred.

"In a minute. Not surprisingly, I'm thirsty. You must be, too. Can I interest you in some water? Wine?"

She looked over her shoulder at him and he rolled onto his side, in the most gorgeous imitation of the famous Burt Reynold pose she'd ever had in her bed. Better than Burt, even. Maybe she should just go back to bed.

"Some water would be good." He nodded.

She stood and suddenly self-conscious of his full-on regard of her bare body, she grabbed her apricot silk kimono off the back of the bedroom door and headed for the kitchen for glasses and ice cubes.

There were interesting things that could be done with ice cubes…

And she should get her thoughts out of the gutter. For God's sake, they were making out like bunnies as it was. They didn't exactly need help. But still…

She let her mind go there, to all the things she would do to that gorgeous hunk of maleness in her bed as she went down the hall to the kitchen. A cool breeze met her at the entrance to the great room and the curtains over the broad sliding glass door stirred as if they breathed.

She stopped, but all the little hairs on the back of her neck stood on end. She scanned the room. Cream couch dimmed by darkness, the blue chairs turned dark gray. The hardwood floor gleaming in the intermittent light exposed by the curtain over the open door.

Something was off, but she couldn't put a name to it.

Silly. It had to be her old paranoia raising its head. She was home. She was safe. Sy was with her. Still, she should have closed the slider before they went to bed. She'd close it before returning to the bedroom.

She padded barefoot into the kitchen and took two glasses from the fridge, ran water from the tap and meanwhile clattered ice cubes into each glass from the fridge dispenser.

The darn hinky feeling didn't go away.

She turned with her back to the sink and faced the room, fighting back the feeling that someone was watching.

But that was silly. It had to be silly.

This was her home. She was safe here—especially with Sy.

By the couch were the plates from their dinner and their half-finished wineglasses. She should clean them up.

She went around the kitchen island and stopped.

Someone had taken the last of the unfinished ribs that she and Sy had left in the foil pan and had dragged them across her lovely white wool rug. The last barbeque sauce had been poured over them so the ribs looked like they sat in a pool of blood.

Cat froze, then spun around, taking in the room again. Someone had been here. In her house. While she and Sy were making love. What else had they done? They could still be here. They could be slitting Sy's throat as she stood here dithering.

She backed up one step. Another.

Across from her the curtain billowed inward.

Old fear inundated her and it was hard to breathe. Leave the door and return to Sy? Kyle Redburn could be out there. He could be coming back right now!

She wanted to scream. She wanted to run down the hall to the safety of Sy. She wanted to call a warning, but if Kyle Redburn was already in the house, that would warn him.

And she wasn't a shrinking violet anymore. She was Artemis, the huntress. The goddess would never run and hide, or take her strength from another being. She was complete in her knowledge that she was celestially blessed and strong.

Gritting her teeth, Cat hiked her robe up, then made a dash for the billowing curtain. She yanked it aside and grabbed the glass door. Shoved it until its fold flattened and the edges locked into place. She sagged against the glass, her breathing ragged. But she'd done it.

Outside the moonlight lit the verandah, turning her wicker furniture black as cast iron. Beyond the glassed-in railings, her yard spilled down the hill under the night-blackened apple tree to the shadowed tangle of blackberry. Something moved in the shadows, then stepped forward into the moonlight.

Cat's breath caught in her throat as Kyle Redburn turned his face to catch the light.

She backed up and backed and backed until the kitchen island blocked her. Then she turned and ran, slamming into her bedroom.

Sy lounged, legs crossed at the ankles, on his back on the bed. Pillows were mounded behind his head and shoulders.

"Hey," he said smiling up at her. Then the smile melted and reshaped to concern. He sat up. "Cat? What's wrong?"

"H—he's here. Kyle Redburn. In the backyard. He's been in the house, too." She was shaking so hard she could barely put two words together.

Sy was off the bed and beside her in an instant, pulling on his shorts to go commando.

"Where?"

"By the blackberries. He left us something on the living room floor. I guess he was trying to get my attention."

And he'd done it. She felt close to crying.

"He's not in the house?"

She shook her head. Then Sy's strong arms came around her and pulled her in close. For a moment she clung to his safety but then, fighting for resolve, she pushed away.

"No. I can't be afraid anymore. This has got to end."

10

The room was quiet except for the quick jerky breaths of the defiant woman before him. The space was all shadows and darkness except for dim light through the curtain, and while darkness might be frightening, it could also be a balm and offer someplace to hide. For that reason he didn't flick the bedroom lights on. He needed to get out there and catch the bastard who had made Cat Moore afraid.

Cat had filled his arms and his senses with something he could only equate with new life. He wanted to pull her into his chest again. For a woman who had confined herself for the past two years, it was as if their lovemaking had unlocked every door inside him. All the regrets. All the guilt he'd felt in the long immortal life he'd lived since Persephone came to him. All the lust and hate and greed he'd felt before his original death, washed through him and were gone. They were subsumed by growing feelings for this small, blonde woman with the eyes of a doe.

Love? It was so much more than the lust and need he was familiar with. This was concern, and tenderness and desire and a blooming feeling in his chest that was almost too much for his chest to hold. But it couldn't be love, could it? He'd committed himself to protecting the land and its denizens. He didn't have time for love of a woman.

"You can do this," he said and gently crooked a finger along her cheek, then tipped her face up to his. "Anyone who can live what you lived through has the strength to do anything they put their mind to. You already proved that he wasn't going to hold you a prisoner any longer. You came outside for the cougar. You came outside to meet me at the refuge. You even went outside to the beach. That isn't the action of someone afraid."

Her gaze met his and seemed to search there, even in the darkness. Then she nodded. "Thank you. Thank you for believing me."

He glanced to the door. "How about showing me where he is?"

He caught her hand and together they retraced their path down the hall, but this time instead of abandon, it was caution they carried. At the entry to the great room, he pulled her to a stop. The two glasses on the kitchen island caught the light through the now-open curtain. The dishes they'd abandoned still lay on the floor, but a dark stain in the middle of the white rug confirmed what Cat had said.

He crossed to the window, Cat at his shoulder, to peer out into the yard. A night wind tossed the cedars in the neighbor's yard and jostled through the leaves of the apple tree. Clouds, passing over the moon, placed roving shadows across the lawn. The blackberries stirred as if something alive walked within them. From the yard next door came the mad ting-ting-ting of wind chimes. Somewhere in the neighborhood a metal clang said a piece of patio furniture blew over.

He undid the lock on the folding glass door. "Don't worry."

He slid open the door and slipped outside onto the patio. After a moment Cat stepped out beside him. She hugged herself as if she was frozen even though the wind was warm.

"He was right there," she said and pointed to a spot on the lawn near the blackberries. Her clear gaze glittered.

"You're certain?" he asked.

She looked at him and her gaze seemed to cloud over. She glanced back to the lawn and them to him again. "I—I'm almost certain." Then her shoulders slumped and she seemed to sag. "He stepped out from the shadows and let me see his face. But who knows. Maybe I'm seeing things. Maybe there was nothing there."

Berating himself for raising her doubts, he shook his head. "I'm going to go take a look. Maybe there'll be marks in the grass." She followed him to the stairs to the yard. "You stay here," he said, turning back to Cat from the top stair. It brought them almost eye-to-eye and he pulled her into him. "The grass'll be damp. No need to get your kimono wet."

A kiss on the lips that lingered a little longer than he'd planned and then he trotted down the stairs.

The grass was cool and damp under his bare feet. It was no longer as long as it had been the day of the cougar, so that was likely another thing that Cat had done. For a woman who had every excuse for horrendous fear, she truly was fighting it—no matter what her friend Jude had told her.

He glanced up at the patio and waved. Loosing long pale fingers from her kimono sleeve, she waved back. The wind caught her blonde hair and tossed it around her face and pressed the length of the silk kimono against her body so she looked as lovely as a tree nymph. Just the thought of that lean, lithe body aroused him again—and he was clearly just a dirty, very old man. Maybe he was only lonely after all these years...

He turned away from the view shaking his head. Who was he kidding? There was something between him and Cat Moore. He only needed to figure out what it was.

He crossed the lawn toward the spot Cat had indicated, careful to use an indirect path so he wouldn't ruin any tracks.

"Here?" he called up to Cat.

"A little to your left."

He took two steps left.

"That's it." Her voice floated down to him.

Scanning the grass revealed nothing. The lawn was too short. He looked up at Cat. "Have you got a flashlight?"

She disappeared into the house for a moment and returned with an emergency flashlight. She hurried down the steps and crossed the grass toward him, hiking up the kimono hem. Her face glowed in the moonlight. Her gaze was filled with fear, but her firm lips and raised chin showed her resolve.

He took the flashlight from her and ran the light over the lawn. A net of dew drops across the grass glittered in the light— except where Cat had said Kyle Redburn had stood. There, the natural net of droplets was mashed together from trampling. A double line of similar smearing led from the blackberry brambles and back. He followed the footprint marks back to the blackberries, Cat right on his heels. The path led around the edge of the yard, keeping to shadow, and then to the backyard gate which stood open. Sy was pretty sure that he'd left it closed behind him.

It was a clear sign that someone had been there.

"So there's some good news and some bad news." He glanced down at her. "The good news is there really was someone there."

She looked up at him. "And the bad news is there really was someone there." She shivered and the hem of her Kimono trailed in the grass behind her. Her throat worked as she swallowed. "Kyle Redburn's come for me."

———

The house had gone cold as winter as Cat sat on the edge of her cream couch and waited for sunrise. The dishes were finally gone from where they'd been left on the floor and the room smelled of carpet cleaner from the attempt to clean up the barbeque stain on the carpet. It hadn't worked. A dull red stain clouded the center of the carpet, or of the room actually. The thunk of the dishwasher closing brought her gaze to Sy. He was fully dressed now, just as she was, though his hair still bore the sexy tousled look of their lovemaking and he still padded silently barefoot.

The police had come and gone. They'd taken a look at the trail in the dew drops and the ribs and barbeque heaped like blood in the center of her great room, taken a few photographs and her and Sy's statements before telling her to be careful and then leaving. They'd said that they'd put extra patrols past her house and that all the police on the Sunshine Coast would be alerted to be on the lookout for Kyle.

None of it left her feeling anymore secure.

Sy left the kitchen and settled beside her on the couch. His strong arms draped her shoulders and he pulled her into the crook of his shoulder.

"It could be worse. I might not have been here."

"He was in my house, Sy. It's bad enough what he's already done to me. He's violated me again and—and—I don't know whether to be afraid or furious."

Sy was silent a moment, then kissed her brow. "Humans are always afraid. I think it's an automatic reaction—fight or flight, and most of us go for flight every time. Personally, if I had a choice, I'd go with furious. It's a lot more powerful. The gods were always furious so everyone else bowed down."

Cat tilted her head up to look at him. "That has got to be the oddest thing you've ever said, but thank you. Furious it is."

She sat forward, leaning her elbows on her knees, then

sprang up to pace around the room. Outside, the sky was lightening, the tops of the tallest cedars and pines blushing as the new sunlight found them. Far out on the water, the waves were tinged with amber.

"I'm going to stop that bastard. I've got to. If I don't, he's either going to kill me or he's going to haunt me and I'm not sure which is worse."

She turned back from the view of the waking day. Sy still sprawled back on the couch, his tan even darker against the cream furniture. He looked sexy as hell, even though dark circles under his worried eyes spoke of his fatigue.

"It's okay, Sy. I can do this. I have to. It's the only way I'm going to have any peace."

"Fury is powerful, but maybe I misspoke. He's already beaten you to within an inch of your life… I don't want anything to happen to you, Cat." He stood and came to her to envelop her in his arms. "There's something about you…"

He tilted her head back and kissed her long and deep. Her body responded, molding against him, but that wasn't what she needed right now. She pulled loose and grinned up at him.

"You may be as dangerous to me as Kyle Redburn. How am I to keep my furious on if you keep distracting me?"

He shrugged. "Well, you won't get hurt with my distractions and I really have become quite fond of you as a complete woman."

She snorted, but then turned away. "I figure we need to get Kyle to come to some place where we can capture him. That's the only way this is ever going to end."

"It's too dangerous, Cat." He caught her shoulders.

She turned in his grasp. "And waiting for him to come for me at a time and place of his choosing isn't?" She shook her head. "Nope. Kyle had it his way by catching me by surprise. It's time the tables were turned. The question is whether you'll help me."

Sy stood immobile, his face a kaleidoscope of emotions that ranged from doubt, concern, and fear. Finally he shook his head.

"I'm sorry, Cat. Given what he did before, I think it's too dangerous. I think you're playing right into his hands. He wants you to go head-to-head with him."

Cat shook her head, certain that Kyle Redburn was more likely playing with her before he returned to finish what he'd started all those years ago. But if Sy couldn't see it…

She stepped away from those welcoming arms and looked up at him. "You saw what he did tonight. I've dealt with people like Kyle all my professional life and with Kyle Redburn for eight years. I know how his mind works—sort of. I know what will draw him out. If you don't believe my assessment, then this isn't going to work. You can't help me, so I think you'd better leave. I have a lot of planning to do."

She motioned him toward the door and he looked from it to her. "Don't do this, Cat. Let's sleep on it and discuss it in the morning."

"It *is* morning, Sy. The first morning of the rest of my life, and I've put off dealing with my situation long enough. Thank you for dinner. Thank you for being here last night. Thank you for the sex, your wise words, and your caring that helped me find myself." She swallowed against the tears that threatened. She truly liked Sy—more than liked. He was a gentleman and brave and smart, not to mention a wonderful lover, and he seemed to care about her. But if he couldn't understand her need to take back her life—well then, he wasn't the right kind of guy for her. It hurt to think it.

It hurt worse to usher him down the hall to the door and yank it open. "I hope we see each other again. We probably will at the refuge."

His mouth opened as if to say something—probably tell her not to come.

She held up a hand. "Be assured that there won't be any

scenes. We're both grown-ups. We have needs. We helped each other out tonight—or at least I like to think we did. I hope."

She smiled up at him, hoping he wouldn't tell her she was a flop in bed because she wanted to have given him pleasure. She'd like the chance to give him more—to make his stern, sad expression blossom in a smile.

He looked down at her and stood too close. "You are one hell of a woman, Cat Moore. The world's a more interesting place with you in it. Please rethink this. Call me if you do. I'll do anything I can to help except set you up for more danger."

His voice was soft and sad. He tilted her head back for one last kiss and her knees almost melted under her at the heat, but damn it, she was not going to be distracted.

She yanked back, breathless. "That is one hell of a weapon."

He tilted a brow at her. "So you'll miss me?"

Miss him. Heck. Even as she opened the door, she didn't want him to leave—ever. But matters with Kyle Redburn had to be dealt with or she'd never be free of him. If Sy didn't want to help her do so, better that he was safely away from her because things were going to get dangerous.

"Have a nice life, Sy Foster." She nodded him out the door.

"Please, Cat. Don't do this."

She shook her head. "The discussion is over."

With regret, she firmly shut the door, locked it, and turned her back on it. Then she retraced her steps into the great room and settled on the couch. God, she missed him already and she hadn't even heard his car leave. The tears flooded through her defenses and she was a fool, sitting here with her nose and eyes dripping and snuffling into a sodden tissue.

What had she done?

What had she done? Sy was about the best thing that had happened to her in a hopelessly long time. Even before Kyle Redburn there hadn't been anyone like Sy in her life. He was strong and good and kind to animals and weird women. He even knew to leave when he was told to, unlike some macho idiots who saw the request to leave as a challenge to their manhood. And Sy was a lover any woman would be lucky to have in her life.

But most of all it was the way he made her feel when he was around her. He didn't even have to be talking to her. He could be busy with his animals and he still seemed aware and attentive to her, too. As if he'd had years of learning how to focus his attention so completely on one thing that now he could provide the same focus for brief microbursts of time so that each person or animal got all of him in that moment. No wonder women loved him.

And she'd sent him away. Damn fool.

11

Sy rested his forehead on his hands as he clutched the truck steering wheel. Overhead the sky blushed with the new day, but the slopes above Davis Bay were still bathed in shadow. Davis Bay would be gray until the sunlight struck it. Then it would turn blue with golden highlights on the crests of the waves, but that was still a good thirty minutes away.

He liked the promise of early mornings, the way the sun caught in the dew and made rainbows. The clean green and ocean scent of the air. The silence except for the rumble of waves and the cries of seagulls, crows, and eagles. The occasional *V* of geese flying over as they sought their feed for the day. It all spoke of life and the important things he'd dedicated this gift of life to protect.

And at the moment, none of them meant anything.

He raised his head and gazed wearily at the house with the blue door.

Damn, Cat Moore. He'd offered to be there for her. He'd told her cared for her—more than he'd ever given away to any other woman—and still she'd rejected him in favor of her damned self-destructive desire to fight this mad man!

Couldn't she see that what she was planning was suicide?

Well, who was he to stop a woman from getting herself killed. He had never wanted to get involved in the first place. He should be back at the refuge caring for the animals, not sitting here mooning over Cat Moore's rejection.

He twisted the key in the ignition and the engine roared to life. He dropped the truck in gear, and without a look at the house, he rolled on by. Cat Moore was on her own from here on out and good luck to her.

He pulled a U-turn and headed back down the street, past the house without looking, and down the hill.

He was free now.

Just as he should be.

But he couldn't seem to breathe past the twisted tightness in his chest.

At the refuge he parked and stepped out into the hushed quiet of the forest. From the sheds came the cooing of pigeons and the chittering of the young squirrels. He aimed for the office and nodded hello to Jana.

She stopped her typing. "Long time no see. Where you been, Boss-man?"

"None of your business." He stomped into his office, grabbed his coveralls, and left with them and a pair of boots tucked under his arm.

"Been to see anyone in particular, Boss?" she called.

"Shut up."

As the door shut behind him, he heard the damned woman chuckling. What the hell did Jana know? Interfering woman. What the hell was she doing coming into the office so early, anyway? Everyone, from the gods on down, had to meddle in his life and he didn't need it.

He snagged a foot pulling the coveralls on and was forced to hop in place like a fool until he could tug his work boots off and slide on the gumboots. He'd have liked to have blamed Jana for the trouble, but it was no one's fault but his own. Instead of changing his shoes in his office like he usually did, he'd stormed out here and this was what he got.

He'd done it to himself with Cat, too. Interfering idiot that he'd been. He should have rescued the cougar and let Jana have her fun with the newbie volunteer. It hadn't killed Cat to get wet cleaning the bat shed. Just like it wouldn't kill him.

Still fuming, he strode up the hill, into the bat shed. The pungent odor of bat guano assaulted his nose. The dim light momentarily blinded him, but thin streamers of light came through the venting high up on the wall. Entering each cage, he used a snow shovel to scrape the concrete floor clean. His shoulders strained. He bent his back into it and enjoyed the sensation. It felt good to put his body through honest physical labor.

Unlike the pleasurable labor of the night before.

Cat's sleek skin came to mind. As did the slow slide into her and her passionate response.

His chest filled with the recollection and how she'd fit so perfectly in the cleft of his shoulder so that he'd wanted to stay together like that for another millennium. The way the sunlight hit her hair. The way the moonlight had filled her gaze as she moved above him. Hell, the way she moved, period.

It was like he feasted on watching her and now he'd set the feast away.

And felt ravenous and starving.

He could phone her. Apologize. He should.

"Fer God's sake." He checked the time on his phone. "It's only been two hours since I left her." After so many years of abstinence, he didn't like the yearning. Hell, he didn't like the weakness in the knees he felt at the thought of never seeing her again.

And that was stupid. How many people had he known who were long dead and lost to him. Some he had even cared for.

But not loved.

He jerked upright from shoveling the last load of guano into a garbage bin for destruction and disposition.

Loved?

No way in Zeus's creation was that possible. He wasn't built that way. Yes, in his first life he'd taken pleasure in women. He'd even taken a wife and various lovers, but love? The idea of it was foreign. In the normal short lifespan of man, it was every man, woman, and child for him- or herself. You might share your time with them, but really you only truly cared for yourself. Love implied that the other person was just as important as you were. Perhaps even more important and that you'd do anything possible to help them and protect them.

He set the shovel by the door and stepped outside into cool morning sunlight. He was sweating, and though the bat shed had been close, it didn't completely account for his perspiration.

Nope, his idiot mind was worrying at something like a bone because what if he hadn't done the right thing by walking away?

It was what Cat had wanted him to do. She'd all but chased him out the door with a broom.

He'd done what she wanted. It was all he could do.

"You keep telling yourself that," he muttered as he trudged down the hill to the raptor cages. He had to get the cougar pen ready, too. The young female cougar was healing well and would need larger living quarters soon.

The soft rasp of the eagle and the rustle of feathers greeted him at the raptor cages. They were built off the side of a log building that held freezer and fridges filled with the bird's feed. The cages were of mesh wire and long and wide enough for the birds to stretch their wings. Each cage had natural branches that formed perches for the residents both in the sun and in the shade. At the moment most of the birds were back under the overhang at the rear of the cages. The large eyes of the owls tracked his movements as he went into the feed storage area. He pulled out dead rodents for each of the residents.

From outside came the rustle of wings and soft, rasped calls. They knew he was coming.

He stepped outside and the birds hopped across perches to the front of the cages.

"Don't worry," he said affectionately. "I've got your orders right here."

He took a cleaver, and using a heavy chopping block at the side of the building, cut the rodent carcasses down to suitable sizes. He set pieces in trays to thaw a little before feeding, pulled on heavy gloves, and used a side gate to step inside and set to cleaning cage floors. The birds protested as he shifted from cage to cage, but settled quickly when he was done invading their individual space. Then he slid the platters of food into each cage and the birds fluttered and swooped down from their perches. Some grabbed a tasty morsel and flew back up to their perch to eat, their sharp beaks and claws shredding the meat.

Another set of needs met. He stripped off his gloves.

Cat had had needs last night. She'd had needs he couldn't meet and so she'd asked him to leave.

"Dammit all to Hades, get out of my head!"

Falling back from the cages, he ran his hands through his hair and stood looking out through the forest. The sunlight placed columns of gold through the trees. The sunbeams struck moss on branches or huckleberry bushes growing on the moldering body of a fallen forest giant, its trunk long since turned to rich, loamy cellulose. He loved this place, this light, this view. It was like he was young again in the spring of the world before humans had caused so much change. Then he'd been the agent of change— always to his benefit.

Now he was futilely trying to preserve a small portion of what these people didn't even realize they were losing and could never get back once it was lost. Like innocence.

He shook his head and turned back to the buildings.

Cat had lost her innocence when Kyle Redburn had beaten her. No one had been there to help her except for the homeless woman who had called for help.

And she was in that situation again. If Kyle Redburn came for her, who would help her this time?

Sy sighed.

He would. He definitely would.

And that meant that he had to go back and make amends for leaving and help her go through with her crazy plans.

He slammed back into the administration building, ignored Jana's tilted eyebrow, and tromped into his office. He closed the door, pulled off the gumboots and coveralls and hung them up. Then he laced up his work boots.

He left his office, ignored the sheaf of pink message slips Jana held up for him, and went out to his truck.

"You sure you should be doing this?" Jana called from behind him. "Get this sorted out, would you! You're letting things slide."

Letting things slide was what he'd done with Cat. The refuge was a business. A charity. Not something that simply ran itself. He needed to attend to it or it would fail. Not swoon around like some lovesick puppy.

It was no place for lovelorn castoffs.

Dammit, he wasn't a castoff and he wasn't lovelorn. He simply had a conscience and couldn't *in good conscience* leave a woman alone to fend for herself in light of the danger she was in.

"Downright heroic," said a little voice in his head that might be Zeus or maybe his conscience.

Complete baloney.

In his truck, he headed back down the hill and nearly hit a silver Prius turning off the Porpoise Bay Road up the hill toward the refuge. He pulled to the side to allow the car to pass, but then realized that the driver looking up at him was Cat.

He rolled the driver's side window down and she slowed and stopped. Then the driver's door opened and Cat leapt out.

"Sy! I—I—we need to talk." She walked back to his truck but didn't approach the window.

On Porpoise Bay Road a car sped past, dappled by the tall trees to either side of the pavement. Sy inhaled the tang of its exhaust overlaid on the scent of trees. Otherwise the air was cool and the sound of running water from the nearby creek was a delightful counterpoint to the wind in the trees and the clapping of leaves that were showing the tarnish of summer heat. He shoved open his door to climb out and face her.

"Yeah. We do." He closed the door and leaned back against the truck fender, waiting for what she had to say. Just seeing Cat filled him with longing and frustration. What would he have become if he had met her millennia ago in Ephyra? What kind of man would he have been? Would his kingdom be long remembered for his positive kingship? Or would he have treated her poorly and still have spent an eternity shoving a stone up a hill in futile labor?

Somehow, he didn't think so. There was something about Cat Moore that made him think of greater things. Being a better man than he had ever been. Even now, though he had dedicated this life to preservation, he had more or less turned his back on humankind connections. Cat had, too. But she didn't like it. Look what it had done to her. The isolation was killing her— would kill her through its agent Kyle Redburn.

Cat sidled from foot to foot as if uncertain where to begin.

"Let me help you. It was a stupid thing for you to do, insisting I leave."

She looked up as if to argue, but he held up his hand. "Only outdone by the stupidity of me actually leaving."

The tension in her shoulders relaxed a little, but there were lines of anxiety around her eyes. Finally, she nodded.

"Stupid is a good word. But I can't let this go on, Sy. You have to understand."

He sucked back all of his macho, protective instincts. "I'm trying. I was just heading back to your place to explain and hopefully find a way around this difference of opinion. There's too much at stake." He motioned to the connection between them.

Her gaze widened slightly and he saw her throat work. "Okay… I know it was unexpected. I keep telling myself that it was simply the emotions of the moment. I was overwrought." A guardedness had come into her voice. "But I heard what you had to say about trying to take on Kyle Redburn alone. You were right. I'd be stupid to try it."

The admission was at least something, but the overwrought thing…

"Are you suggesting that the only reason we made love was because you'd been upset by seeing Kyle?"

She spread her hands a little. "It makes sense, doesn't it? People sleep together for reasons like that all the time. Emotions and tensions run high and they need release. It's a reasonable explanation."

Those clear brown eyes, that expressive pink mouth that he had tasted and devoured not that long ago.

In one step he was across to her and caught her in his arms. He kissed her—hard—and her lips parted to him. She melted into his chest and suddenly was plastered to him, one leg slung around his hip as if she, like he, could not get enough. When he was done ravaging her mouth, he pulled back a little.

"You mean that kind of tension release?"

Brown eyes blinked up at him and she hummed a little yes in her throat. Then she leaned up and trailed kisses from his mouth, along his jaw, and down his throat. A passing car honked.

Sy waved them off and picked Cat up. She wrapped her legs around him and he cupped her bum so they were eye-to-eye.

"Stupid fight?" he asked.

"It was," she nodded.

"Made up?" he asked.

"Oh, God, yes." She leaned in for another lingering kiss. "Double yes," she said when they both came up for air.

"Good." He let her slip to the ground and steadied her. "So I've been thinking about this Kyle Redburn problem…"

———

With the sunlight and the forest dappling his almost black hair, Sy Foster had to be the most beautiful man Cat had ever seen. Not to mention sexy. Of course, maybe it was the way his arms held her so gently, or the clean scent of cedar and soap and water that came from his skin and clothing. And then there was the substance of him: the height, and the breadth of his shoulders. The way his shirt hung loose around his narrow hips. The muscled thighs she'd wrapped her legs around last night. Lean muscle and strength, that was Sy Foster. And then there was the innate kindness that had brought him to her door last night and the tenderness he'd shown her. Not to mention the passion.

Oh, the passion. Remembered heat pulsed through her as he held her close. The shadowed trees were his perfect environment. She could picture him running naked through the great green sword ferns and mossy boulders. He would be a great warrior for the land and animals.

For her?

She ran her palm down his cheek, rough from lack of shaving. He must have come directly to the refuge from her place.

"You have to understand. All my life I was strong enough to overcome anything I faced. I never asked for help from anyone. And then Kyle happened and it was even harder to ask. I'm sorry

I pushed you away. It was the last thing I wanted." She couldn't look him in the eyes. "I—I kinda like you, Sy Foster."

His chuckle rumbled through his chest as he pulled her against him. "It's mutual, Cat Moore. Now how do you want to get rid of this ghost from your past? 'Cause I was thinking about it while I was working off my tantrum at being none-too-gently cast from your house."

He nodded down at her. "Yes, a tantrum. I was right pissed off that you asked me to leave. Cleaning cages is the perfect time for reflection. I realized that you were right. You have to do this or you won't ever have a life. So you said that you want to set a time and place for Kyle to come to you. I wondered whether the refuge might do—as the place."

She nodded slowly. "It might work. Frankly, it would be a godsend. The thought of luring him into my home freaked me out."

"Then consider it done. Let's head up and we can conspire with Jana. If there's anyone who can come up with nefarious plots, it's her. She's been setting me up to accidentally meet women for years."

After another toe-curling kiss, Sy turned his truck around and followed her silver Prius up the road to the refuge. They parked and he ushered her inside the administration building.

Jana sat, hands folded on her desk. She took in the way Sy's arm came around Cat'sshoulders and her jaw worked. "Now isn't this a pretty picture. That didn't take very long, oh fearless leader. And by your expression, you're going to be nicer to be around this time."

Cat glanced up at him. "You mean you were unpleasant to poor Jana?"

"I had other things on my mind, and don't you two try tag-teaming me." He wagged a finger under both their noses and Cat burst out laughing.

So did Jana. "Wouldn't think of it, Boss-man."

Sy hauled two chairs over to Jana's desk. "So. We have a problem, Jana, and we'd like your help solving it."

She looked from Cat to Sy, her expression calculating. "Relationship counseling is not my forte."

Cat looked to Sy and they both grinned.

"Who said we need counseling? It's your plotting skills we need," Sy began. Then he told her about their problem.

When he was done, the morning was almost gone and Jana's expression had turned grim. She shook her head. Other volunteers had come, signed in, and gone.

Jana met Cat's gaze. "I can't believe you've been through all that—and that some people are like that. The guy must be—I don't know what—would you call him crazy?"

"Angry, more like," Cat said and sighed. "He was angry when I first met him and nothing's changed—except maybe he's gotten more dangerous. I knew he was unstable, but I never figured it was like this. Unfortunately, he seems to have fixated on me as the source of his problems. Now I have to stop him."

Jana arched a brow and chewed her lips for a moment as if she assessed Cat anew. Then she turned to Sy.

"You know, I think I can see why she's the one. How can someone who has been through so much still be so strong? No wonder you're attracted. No wonder you want to help her. I will, too."

She turned back to Cat. "So, what are you thinking?"

"When he attacked me, he surprised me at a time and place of his choosing. I want to set things up so that he tries it again, but I want it to be where and when I decide."

Jana sat back in her chair looking thoughtful. "Tall order." She shook her head. "From what I gather, you don't go out much. Have I got that right?"

Cat felt herself color slightly, wondering just how she'd given that fact away. Sy had probably said something. "When I came here the other day, it was almost the first time I'd been out since I moved here. I've been depending on home delivery services…"

And she felt so damn stupid that she'd let it go so far; and yet, if she'd been simply living an ordinary life, she wouldn't be here on the coast, she wouldn't have met Sy, and Kyle Redburn would likely have already found her and finished the job. Being a shut-in might have saved her.

Jana's gaze went faraway as she tapped her fingers on her desk. Then she shook herself and grinned. "Seems to me that the refuge makes the perfect spot to do this thing. You volunteer here and start coming in the late afternoon. We can set it up that it looks like everyone leaves before you so you'll be alone, but Sy and I can head to that shack of Sy's up in the bush and keep in touch by walkie-talkie. When your guy comes, we can be back here in the blink of an eye." She looked from Cat to Sy. "Whaddaya think?"

Sy nodded slowly. "That could work. We can make sure there are weapons handy to deal with the guy. A few crowbars and such."

"If that's going to work, let me look at the volunteer schedule and see what I can do." Jana lifted her chin toward the door. "Let me figure this out. You two go have fun."

"You'll want to see the cougar?" Sy said. "She's come a long way in a short time."

Cat followed him out of the admin area and into the veterinary clinic behind the offices. This time he didn't hold her in the observation room. Instead, he took her through a secondary locked door and into the cage room.

The musky scent of cat was the first thing Cat noted. The overhead lighting was dim. The floors and walls were white-painted concrete with examination tables at one end and ranks of variously sized cages across the rear wall. High up, just below the roof trusses, ventilation fans turned slowly, replacing the warm air in the cage room with the cooler, cedar-scented air of the forest.

Sy guided her along the wall across from the cages until they were even with the one that held the lanky form of the young cougar. She lounged on her side, her tawny fur already having regained a healthier glow. Her green-gold gaze locked on them and followed Cat as she moved. A pink tongue licked long black whiskers.

"I feel like prey and she's just working herself up to eating," Cat said.

"She does have a predator's presence," Sy agreed. "But she's alert and the wounds are healing."

"When will she be able to be released?" She glanced up at Sy. He stood considering her question, his hands stuck in his pockets.

"It depends. Could be as early as next week if the wounds don't abscess. Could be a week or two longer if they do. We don't want to release her if it looks like the wounds are healing over but leaving infection internally. But she's ready to use her leg so I think we'll be putting her in a pen tomorrow."

"She is so beautiful," Cat said and stepped closer to the cage.

The cougar yawned and stood, head down, unblinking, studying her. Okay, now she really knew what prey felt like. Actually, she knew what prey felt like all too well. But she was no longer a deer in the forest.

"What are you thinking?" Sy asked, coming up behind her and sliding his hands around her sides.

"That I'm not afraid any longer." She looked up at him. "I mean, I'm afraid of what could happen—it would be stupid not to be. But I'm not going to live my life looking over my shoulder all the time anymore. This is over."

He leaned down to nip her ear and a delicious tremor ran through her.

"You can look over your shoulder at me, anytime," Sy whispered in her ear.

She turned in his arms and met his mouth with hers.

"Thank you for coming back. For being you."

He shook his head and shrugged. "I haven't done anything other than fallen for you."

His words made her feel lucky in so many ways. Maybe this was what they called making lemonade out of lemons.

"Do you think this will work?" She didn't want to allow her doubts to creep in, but...

"It'll work. Jana's worked for me about six years and she's smart and willing to help. Between her and me, consider yourself safe. And just to make sure, I'm not leaving your side until this is over—other than here at the refuge."

He pulled her into an embrace that felt so right she could almost sigh and relax into it. But not until everyone was safe.

Not until this was over.

12

A week passed and then two. Sy had spent the two weeks living amid the cream sofa and blue chairs and the matching blue view of the ocean at Cat's house. The ocean breeze greeted them each morning when he slid open the folding doors and they drank lattes and ate croissants and fresh summer fruit sitting on the patio watching the tugs haul barges along the inside passage of Georgia Strait. The sun would catch in Cat's honey-blonde hair and he would find himself breathless and unbelieving that he was truly here with this woman. It was as if he had set his sights on a goddess and the goddess had returned his affections. He found himself waiting for her to come to her senses and walk away from him, but so far it hadn't happened.

Each night they fell passionately together in Cat's king-sized bed. Each morning they woke with tender lovemaking that left him breathless and tender-feeling in his chest. He'd come to realize that, strangely, he cared deeply for this woman—more deeply than he had ever cared for anyone. He would do anything for her, including risk his life, and so he was having second thoughts about Cat risking herself to catch Kyle Redburn.

It was a sunny August afternoon when he finally broached

the subject. They were seated on the patio, Cat with her reading visor pulled low over her eyes so he couldn't actually see if she was awake, but she hadn't turned a page in a very long time.

"Cat?"

"Mm-hmm?"

How to say this without getting her dander up. "I've been thinking. Are you sure that we're the best people to do this?"

Cat's blonde head turned. The visor pushed back and a dark brown, narrowed gaze peered out at him from the shadows.

He was blowing it, but he had to get this out. He lowered his voice in case, heaven forbid, Kyle Redburn was somewhere close watching and listening. "I mean Jana and I have our hearts in the right place, but do we really know about taking down a criminal? We could blow this thing and put you at risk by leaving you exposed to Kyle Redburn."

Cat closed her book, her finger holding her place. "And I thought we went over this the day we agreed on what we were going to do." She cast a glance over the verandah railing and also lowered her voice. "I go up there everyday and work in the cage sheds late in the day. You and Jana pretend to leave and everyday we wait. So far there's been no Kyle Redburn. I'm beginning to think I imagined him. It could have been an opportunist kid who dumped the ribs on the carpet. He could have looked up at the house and my mind could have changed his feature's to Kyle's just like when I was walking on the beach." She shook her head. "But I've got to do this, Sy. It's the only way I'll get rid of my demons. Do you understand?"

He nodded, even though he didn't. Apparently being supportive of another person was exceedingly frustrating. Maybe it was a character flaw, but no wonder he hadn't done it when he was king and everyone had to be supportive of him. To his recollection it was far better to be on the receiving end.

He inhaled. "So how long do we continue like this? It's not much of a life for us or for Jana, though she's been a good sport so far. And I know she has family visiting… She might have joined in for the lark of it, but I feel like I'm going to have to start paying her overtime if this goes on much longer."

Cat's gaze stiffened. So did her shoulders. "If you have to pay her, I'll cover the costs. After all, I've had nothing to spend my money on." She flipped the book open. "If this is too hard for you, you don't have to be involved. I can do this on my own."

He stood up and leaned down to her. "Cut the crap, Cat! That's not what I meant. And that's that type of bravado that's going to get you hurt. Or worse yet, killed."

She carefully placed the book on the verandah deck and stood. Then she went through the sliding glass doors inside and turned to face him. He followed her inside.

"So, what? I give up now and let him catch me when I'm off my guard? Or maybe you'd prefer that I live my life clinging to you for safety?"

"Dammit, Cat. You know that's not what I want. I want you healthy and happy. And alive would be good, too. I just think maybe we should alert the police to our little plan, so if we call for help they know it's serious." But that wasn't what he meant at all. He wanted to pack Cat up and whisk her away someplace else. Someplace safe.

Her glare softened a little. "I can agree to informing the police, if that's what it takes for you to let me do this." She shook her head. "Let me rephrase: You're not letting me do this. I don't need your permission. But if phoning the police makes you more comfortable backing me up like we planned, then I'm for it."

She stepped up to him and placed her palm softly on his chest. Her brown gaze shifted like shadows under leaves. "I don't want to fight about this, Sy. I care too much about you. About us, but this is something I have to do."

He pulled her into him, reveling in her warmth, inhaling her rose blossom scent as if it was nectar. Gods, let them get through this. He suddenly could imagine himself as Orpheus, begging to return to Hades in the hopes of bringing Cat back to life. Whatever it took, he would keep Cat safe. He would get her through this.

———

Four thirty and this late in August, though the sun was hidden behind the trees, the windless air down below at the refuge was hot and stifling. The animals knew it. They remained quiet in their cages, most dozing through the late summer heat, including the cougar who had been moved from the isolation of the smaller administration building cages out to a large enclosure that included bushes in the corners and a stack of logs that she could lounge on. In the heat today, that was exactly what she was doing, her green-gold eyes at half-mast, absolutely still except for a slight twitch of the dark tip of her tail.

Cat stood outside the enclosure as had become her habit on these long afternoons. It was closed and off-limits to all but the veterinarian, and Sy kept the tours of tourists and visitors away.

"Hey beautiful. You almost ready to go free?"

The cougar's tail flicked a little faster.

"I hear rumors that you might be gone at the end of the week."

The cat lifted its head and yawned, revealing gleaming white teeth, then stood and turned around to leave Cat facing the animal's hindquarters. "Well, I guess I know what you think of me."

She sighed and shrugged, then trudged up the slope to the bat shed carrying her gum boots. The darn place had been part of her routine since they'd started this ruse. So had the raptor cage. At the raptor cage there was the cleaver as a weapon. At the bat shed they had placed a crowbar against the rear wall of the building so that Cat would have a weapon to hand in case Kyle Redburn attacked.

In the heat it all seemed a tad futile. Kyle apparently wasn't coming or was biding his time.

Just the walk up to the shed left her sweating even though she was only wearing shorts and a singlet under the coveralls. Toeing off her shoes, she pulled on the boots, then tugged open the top of the coveralls and removed her arms from the sleeves. She tied them around her waist and set her cell phone and car keys in her shoes before stepping inside.

The dusty-sweet scent of bat guano struck her nose and she coughed, then cleared her throat and stepped inside, her feet sliding in the slightly oversized gumboots.

Her entrance set off a froth of movement through the bats in the rafters. High pitched shrieks and twitters filled the air, almost beyond hearing. From the rear wall she grabbed the hose and turned on the water.

The high-pressure hose bucked in her hands as she sluiced water over the floor. When she had everything damp, she left the hose nozzle turned off by the water faucet and grabbed the shovel and used it to scrape the concrete free of guano, shoving the debris into the waste trough/gutter at the end of the building. When she was done, she paused to ease her back and look up at the bats. The small flying foxes were mostly asleep, leathery wings cocooning their bodies. A few peered down at her with dark, beady eyes.

She grinned up at them. "Sure do wish you guys could figure out to poop at one end of the building. It would make my job a lot easier."

Of course, no one answered and she found herself whistling tunelessly as she used the broom to sweep the debris down the trough and out of the building. Just a final hose down and she'd be done.

The door squeaked open and bumped behind her.

"I'm just about done here," she said as she leaned the broom in the corner. She just needed to reclaim the hose nozzle. She glanced over her shoulder, expecting Sy to be waiting for her because he too-often found an excuse to come down to her.

A man stood there, broader shouldered than Sy. Tall, but with scraggly straight hair almost down to his shoulders. He wore jeans, a faded green t-shirt, and a denim jacket that strained around his muscle-bound arms.

Not Sy.

All the little hairs on her body stood on end.

"Hello, Catherine. Long time, no see. Or I should say you haven't seen me, though I've seen plenty of you." Kyle Redburn took a step forward and grinned.

Cat edged back a step while everything else seemed frozen. Get away. Get away. Get away played over and over in her head, but she couldn't get herself to move. Instead she floated somewhere above her head, watching what was about to happen.

"What's this, little kitty-cat? I can call you that, right? We've known each other for so long—had such an impact on each other's lives. You ruined mine, so I aimed to give it back, tit-for-tat. Imagine my surprise when I find out that you seem to have come out of it okay." He shook his head and advanced another step.

Cat jerked back into her body and leapt back. The crowbar. They'd put it in the corner by the broom.

The shed's log wall dug into her spine. Left and right were the wire cages. There was nowhere to go but forward and Kyle blocked the way to the door.

Terror had her hands spidering along the wall timbers seeking the broom, the crowbar, anything that might be a weapon. She glanced down, but the crowbar she'd avoided every day for the past two weeks no longer stood in the shadow.

Where? Who took it away?

She looked back at Kyle and his triumphant smile. Her hands scrambled behind her and came up against a rubber coil.

Hose.

Maybe…

She grabbed it, brought it in front of her, and squeezed the nozzle. A high-pressure water stream slammed into Kyle. He staggered back, slipped on the damp concrete, and went down hard on his ass against the left-hand cage. She kept the hose on him and leapt over his legs for the door.

His roar filled the shed as she fumbled the latch, slammed it open, and fled.

Uphill. Gumboots slopping onto the forest trail in the fading light of late afternoon. Ferns swept at her feet. Spruce branches caught in her hair as she stumbled into the woods. Found the trail.

"Sy!" she screamed and kept on running. The cabin where Sy and Jana waited was farther uphill in the forest. She'd visited it once with Sy. It was a simple log cabin that he'd built with his own hands when he'd first come to the Sunshine Coast. He'd started caring for injured animals there, and out of that expertise had grown the refuge, though the original cabin was rarely used now.

Just get there.

She glanced over her shoulder and Kyle's furious face was too close for comfort. She redoubled her speed, but the damn gumboots were about the farthest thing from running shoes she could have on and the coveralls tied around her waist kept catching on things. She hiked up the tied sleeves and kept running. Another check behind her and she'd put a little more distance between her and Kyle. She could do this. Just get to Sy and this would be over.

Something snagged her feet and she went down.

Hard. Hands and knees scraped. Dazed, she came up. A wire gleamed, strung across the path, and Kyle was coming.

Who? Why?

She struggled up and looked up the trail. If one wire was here, who knew how many more were there. She ducked sideways into the woods, shoving through sword ferns and huckleberry brush, ducking under lichen-draped branches. Behind came the crunch and crash of Kyle following her. She rushed through the brush, praying she could keep her lead. Ahead was a thick line of willow and ferns. An old, moss-laden, tree stump provided a nursery for two young pine trees.

She glanced back and there was no sign of Kyle. She headed for the brush and shoved blindly through. Her foot came down on emptiness.

She fell.

Tumbling down the steep undercut side of a ravine, she slammed her side into a tree. Her knee hit a rock and pain shot up her leg. She landed hard in a dry, gravel streambed and lay there a moment catching her breath. Then she scrambled up because Kyle couldn't be allowed to see where she was.

Pain drove up her leg. Her knee gave, and she bit back a moan but kept going. Her breath sobbed as she hobbled over to the ravine wall where, hopefully she would be harder to see.

She huddled there gasping. Where was Sy? Why hadn't he answered? She didn't dare call for help now. Feeling helpless and alone, she crouched down amid the ferns and pulled them half over her. She could wait here for help.

But her knee throbbed, and if she didn't keep moving, it was going to stiffen. If Kyle found her, she'd stand no chance at all. Besides, standing up to Kyle was her task and her task alone. Maybe Sy had decided not to help her. Or maybe Kyle had taken out Sy and Jana.

Rejecting that possibility, she stood and tested her injured leg. Pain was a jagged edge at each movement, but the knee held. So she'd worry about the pain later. Time to get moving and stop feeling sorry for herself. She needed to get back to the admin building and call for help.

Following the ravine and trying to keep to its undercut upper edge, she climbed over rocks, old tree roots, and tangles of branches that had been deposited in previous years' spring runoff. A jagged branch gouged her forehead and blood trickled into her eye. Great. Another scar. Nothing she could do anything about for now. The farther she went, the more painful her leg throbbed.

The late afternoon light was fading when a faint game trail up the side of the ravine stopped her. There were deer who sometimes came to graze the small lawn and the rhododendrons planted around the refuge. This could be their trail.

It was a steep bit of mud, now dried and trampled to loose earth. Not an easy climb for a woman with only one good leg, but that couldn't be helped. Using the ferns and small trees that clung tenaciously to the ravine sides, she started up. Her good leg slipped and pain shot up her injured knee. She moaned and clung to a pine trunk, waiting for the pain to subside enough to keep going. When she swiped at her face, her hand came away bloody.

After the pain subsided, she kept going, creeping up the ravine until suddenly she found flat forest before her. A thin screen of young poplar and blackberry brambles hid her from the refuge buildings, but the amber parking lot lights had come on as the light failed. She hesitated, but there was no sign of Kyle and the animals showed no sign of being disturbed. She caught a whiff of animal droppings as an undertone to the omnipresent cedar.

After a few minutes, she cautiously pushed through the brambles, stopped, and waited. There was no sign of anyone.

She limped across the open ground to the admin building and inside through the unlocked main door. At Jana's desk she picked up the phone handset. No dial tone. Of course… she punched an outgoing line.

The line stayed silent.

What the…

She tried another line. Another. All five lines stayed silent.

Damn. Kyle must have disabled the phone. That left her cell, but coverage was spotty at the best of times here at the refuge. But if she got her phone, she'd have her keys as well. She could go for help.

She stepped outside. Across the parking lot, her little silver car beckoned. Uphill, she scanned the cage and pathways. No one was there. Maybe Sy and Jana simply hadn't heard her calls.

Or else Kyle had gotten to them first.

A sick feeling flooded the pit of her stomach. That couldn't be the case. She wouldn't let her mind go there. Surely Kyle couldn't have overpowered them both… She'd have heard something.

But she had been using the power hose. The water made it hard to hear anything else.

Well, she couldn't do anything about it at the moment. She had to get help for all of them and that meant getting her shoes, phone, and keys. And she needed a weapon. They'd left another crowbar in Sy's office. She retrieved it and, fighting the limp, she hurried up the hill and was almost to the bat shed when a figure appeared on the path.

Cat almost leapt away until she realized the person was small —almost her size.

"Jana?" she called softly.

"Cat! There you are. I've been looking for you." Jana shoved her thick hair back behind her ears and grinned. "Where *have* you been? You look like you'd been in a war."

Cat ignored the comment about her looks, dropped the crowbar, and caught Jana in her arms. "Thank God you're all right. I've been worried sick. Where's Sy? Is he okay?"

"All right? Of course I'm all right. Sy's back at the cabin waiting for you, of course. I thought I'd wander down and make sure everything was all right." Another of Jana's sharp grins.

Cat shook her head. "Kyle's here. He nearly caught me in the bat shed but I got past him and headed up toward the cottage and then into the woods. I came down here to use the phone and call for help." She leaned down to reclaim her shoes, keys, and phone.

"Cell phones don't have very good reception, you know."

Cat glanced up at Jana and nodded, pulled off the overlarge gumboots, and slid her feet into her sneakers—thankfully much cooler and they fit. She pulled out her phone and tried 9-1-1. Nothing happened.

"Told you," Jana said and picked up the crowbar. "Now come on. I'll take you to Sy and you can try the phone farther up. It might work there."

Jana led off at a rapid pace that Cat was forced to match. It took all of her effort and she was puffing against the pain after the fifteen-minute march up the hillside while keeping an eye out for Kyle in the darkening forest.

Sy's old cabin stood in a clearing in the trees, but in the sun and rain of the west coast weather, the forest was gradually taking back the clearing again. In the evening gloom of the forest, young poplar trees fringed the clearing, and Scotch broom, heavy with seed pods, stood disheveled inside the ring of trees. Grass as tall as her knees grew alongside the cabin walls and up through stacked cages that stood at one side of the structure. The cabin itself looked sturdy and hunkered against what the world threw at it, even though its door looked warped and slightly off-true and the lone window beside the door was cataracted in thick plastic.

She thought of Sy and smiled. At times he seemed to have the same "him against the world" attitude.

The clearing was unnaturally quiet. Sure, it was that odd, dim space between day and night, but even then, there was usually bird song and the hush that comes as the light is stolen. This was more like everything held its breath.

"Sy?" she called, and scanned the clearing. Had Kyle been here while Jana was with her? She turned back to Jana. "Where is he?"

"In the cabin. He must be busy with something. At least that's where I left him," Jana said, coming up beside Cat. Jana drew in a deep breath and smiled. "Nice evening, isn't it. Regardless of stuff going down."

All the little hairs on Cat's body stood on end. Something was off here and Jana was acting downright strange. It was no nice evening when you'd been terrorized and chased and fallen down a ravine. What the heck was Jana thinking? Cat stepped up the two steps to the cabin door.

"Sy?" She pushed the door open.

Everything was shadows inside except for a lighter gray of smeary light from the window and the open door that caught the edge of the rough square table and one chair.

"Sy?" She stepped up inside, the shadows gradually receding as her eyes adjusted. A figure sat in another chair at the rear of the room.

A powerful blow across her back sent her stumbling into the darkness. She fell and rolled in time to see the cabin door slam closed.

"Jana, what the hell's going on?" But she knew she'd been betrayed. Jana had used the crowbar on her. Cat was lucky the weapon hadn't been used on her head. As it was, her ribs screamed when she moved. She got to her knees.

Sy slumped, tied into the upright wooden chair with his hands behind his back and his feet tied to the chair legs. His head hung forward, his midnight hair covering his face and eyes.

"Sy!" She crawled to him.

She and Sy were trapped and Jana had clearly done

something to incapacitate Sy until Kyle's return. She patted Sy's face. He groaned and pulled away.

That was good, wasn't it? He was aware, at least.

She kept one ear alert for Kyle's arrival and leaned over Sy. "Sy! You have to wake up. Please wake up. We have to get out of here. Kyle's coming. You can't be like this or he'll hurt you— worse than you already are."

She stroked his face, ran her fingers through his hair, and found a large bump on the back of his head that told her what had happened to him.

Swiftly she untied the knots on his hands. Did the same at his ankles, but left the ropes at both ankles and wrists loosely looped around him so that a cursory look in this light might fool the eye. Hopefully Sy would wake and be able to save himself because she didn't dare stay where she was.

With the help of Sy's chair, she pulled herself up to standing, then went to the door; but it refused to open. "Jana? Open the door. This isn't funny. You're in a lot of trouble, but it's not too late to do the right thing and let Sy and me go."

A snicker came through the door. "Funny isn't what I was going for, Catherine, so you can quit your oh-so-reasonable probation talk. Payback is more like it. After all these years of ruining people's lives, isn't it time someone ruined yours?"

"What… I don't understand." Her mind felt numb and counterpoint to the pain in her body.

"I'm Kyle's sister, you idiot. You even spoke to me on the phone when you were doing that fucking report for the court. I was living right here, but I guess you forgot that. You ruined Kyle. My baby brother. You set him on the run as a wanted man. And then imagine my surprise when you showed up on one of the ferries when I was coming home from visiting him. I followed you home and that set Kyle and me planning. It only got better when you actually called the refuge and showed up here. Thenyou start moaning about how Kyle Redburn hurt you so much and actually asked me for help. That was rich! It was like the universe was telling me it was time for revenge after all the lording it over Kyle, as if being his probation officer gave you the right to control him. He should have killed you, bitch."

Cat staggered back from the door, her legs like mush. Now that she knew, she should have seen. That was why Jana had looked so familiar when she met her—she had the same facial structure as Kyle. And she should have realized that when Jana found Cat, Jana should have suggested the admin building phones to call for help—unless she knew the administration phones were out—unless she'd been complicit in disabling the phone lines. The only good thing about Cat's situation was that Kyle wasn't here right now.

She left the door and returned to Sy.

"Please, Sy. Please." She kissed him on the lips and felt him respond.

From beyond the wooden walls she heard voices. Jana's higher pitch and something much lower.

Kyle.

"Oh, God, Sy. Wake up. I can't save us if you're like this." And she wanted to save them both, she just wasn't sure how. If she could escape, it would keep Kyle away from Sy if he pursued. That would give Sy a chance.

She hoped.

The voices continued outside. There was triumph and gloating in their tone, though she couldn't distinguish the words. Deciding what to do with them, probably. Well, she, for one, wasn't hanging around to find out what they came up with. The walls were solid and so was the door unless she was a heck of a lot stronger. That left the window.

The heavy plastic was in two layers. One was stapled to the outside of the cabin. The other was stapled to the inside, leaving air for insulation between. Cautiously, she began to pull the staples loose from inside the window until a large, triangular, plastic flap was loosened.

As quietly as possible, she retrieved the other chair from the table and carried it to the window. Standing on it put her at the correct angle, but it was going to be all about timing.

And luck. And sucking up the pain from too many places in her body.

She placed most of her weight on her good leg and waited, flexing her fingers into fists. *Please let this work.* It was taking a terrible risk, going through the window head first, but she really had no choice. She didn't even know what was on the ground outside. She'd find out soon enough.

Through the window, the argument outside was more distinct. Kyle was all for killing them—after he'd had his fun— and leaving the bodies, while Jana thought their remains should be hidden away from the refuge.

"I can tell the police that they were lovers. They could have simply run away together. It's plausible and it will leave me still working at the refuge. We can milk this place for a few months and disappear ourselves," Jana said.

Something cold as stone and twice as hard formed in Cat's stomach. No way was she letting plans like that come true. To save Sy, the first thing was to save herself and then call for help.

The argument died and she wasn't sure who's opinion won, but footfall grated on the wooden front steps. She aimed her fists for the window and inhaled a deep breath.

The lock rattled and clicked and the door swung open as Cat launched herself into the window. The plastic held, but the staples holding it didn't. They ripped from the wood under Cat's momentum and suddenly she was falling head first and tucking her head and rolling. A roar came from behind her as she slammed against something hard and barked the shin of her bad leg.

She came up running and heard Jana yelling.

Ignore the pain and live. Ignore Sy left behind and bring help to save him. Ignore everything except the fear that put wings on her heels and kept her from Kyle.

She ran.

The trail was dark and she stumbled and caught herself against branches and cedar trunks. Behind came Kyle's crashing passage egging her on. Faster. Faster.

If she could make the parking lot, she now had her keys. She could escape to the road and call for help from there. She hauled out her keys in preparation.

The trail sloped down, and ahead, silhouetted against the parking lot lights, she made out the shape of the bat shed. Not far now. She could do this. She could. She was flying down the trail, running with all the strength that fear could give her. Running like she once had run marathons. She pumped her arms and ran faster.

Her foot found a hole. Her ankle twisted. She went down and her keys went flying somewhere into the darkness. She scraped her palms, her knees, but was up again and running. Her breath filled her ears. Her blood pounded through her veins. Pain sang up her leg.

No keys. And the cell didn't work.

The pain screamed through her leg and she was pretty sure that she couldn't keep running much longer. She had to hide. Had to hide and find a place with cell reception. Sometimes it faded in at the admin building.

Stumbling downhill, she looked over her shoulder. Kyle burst out of the brush on the trail and flicked on a flashlight. He'd expect her to head to the admin building. Once she was in there, it was more or less the end of the road. There had to be somewhere else to hide.

She ducked sideways amid the sheds, away from the pool of light by the admin building parking lot, and she was immediately lost in the darkness. She slowed. She couldn't afford another fall like the last one.

"Hey, kitty-cat, where you going now? You gotta know I'm gonna find you and then we're going to play, play, play." Kyle's voice rang eerily through the dark forest and refuge, followed by his low chuckle.

Cat shivered and looked wildly around her. There had to be somewhere to hide. She already knew his play. This time she wouldn't survive.

She staggered into a fence and followed it along, holding to the wire to relieve weight from her bad leg. A musky odor filled her nose and she realized where she was.

She looked back up the hill, where Kyle whistled as he searched for her. Maybe. Just maybe…

At the gate to the cougar cage, she swiftly undid the combination lock, thanking the gods that she had watched Sy open the cage so many times that she'd learned the numbers. She ducked inside and looked left and right. No sign of the cougar. But the darn lock was impossible to reattach from the inside. She pocketed the lock and stumbled farther into the pen. She could maybe hide in the den built for the cougar along the rear wall, but something stopped her. If she was looking for someone, that was the first place she'd check.

"Kitty-cat, oh kitty-cat. Come out, come out, wherever you are!"

His voice seemed to come from the administration building that was only one shed away. She stumbled around the tangle of logs in the center of the pen to the rear corner where a clump of brush had been left standing. She'd seen the cougar use it for shade from the sun. She'd use it to hide now. At the bushes she used a stick to poke inside. There was no hiss or growl. The cougar was somewhere else.

She crawled inside, half-dragging her bad leg, and sat there panting. The pain throbbed through her and she could feel the heat in her knee. How long she could stay here, she didn't know. Certainly in daylight she'd be seen. She thought she was safe from Kyle's flashlight, though.

As if formed from her thought, a flashlight flared across the ground around the nearby raptor shed. The birds rasped and she heard wings thump against the walls. Nights were usually quiet around here.

But not tonight. Kyle's figure appeared around the corner of the shed. Lit eerily by the flashlight's backwash, his face was skeletal and predatory. She froze where she was.

"Come out, come out, wherever you are! Kitty-cat, you can't hide forever. Kyle's going to get angry if he has to look too hard and you know that means he'll have to be harder on you."

God, the guy was talking about himself in third person. Didn't that mean he was disassociating? There was no way she could expect him to act like a human being. Or maybe she could —the very worst kind of human.

She fought back a whimper and clutched her knees more tightly to her chest. It only made the pain worse. She had to figure that, with this injured leg, if she stayed here too long, the only way she'd get out of here was if someone carried her.

Kyle reached the cougar pen and sent the flashlight's glare across the enclosure.

Cat cringed back and ducked her face away from the light. Nothing moved in the pen.

Kyle swung the light around the surrounding area. Forest beyond the cougar pen. More sheds stood uphill. The light came back to the cougar enclosure and the sign on the cage that said closed from viewing. The light slid to the gate and the closure. No lock.

He flipped the closure and opened the gate to step inside.

Oh God, he was going to search the cage. He'd find her. Carefully, she slid her legs under her and almost screamed at the pain in her knee. If he left the gate open, maybe she could wait until he was on the other side of the cage. Maybe she could outrun him to the gate. She could slam it closed and lock it behind her.

Lock him in.

Puffing through her mouth to exhale the pain, she watched him through the leaves. He closed the gate behind him, but it wasn't locked. She could still get free if she was fast.

If her leg would work.

At the rear of the cage was the alcove built to provide the cougar with a den in the cold and rainy season. Anyone could expect that she might hide in there. Kyle took the bait and headed right for it, skirting around the heap of logs.

Cat sucked in a deep breath, but still felt breathless. She had to do this. She'd done it before, outrunning him from the cabin.

But that was before her second fall, before she'd had a chance to stiffen up here.

She waited until Kyle was as far away as possible and was bent over, flashing his light inside the den. She threw herself up and forward, springing down beside the logs, running for the gate. Her bad leg gave and she hobbled on. Heard Kyle's shout and his stumble over the logs to reach her. She made the gate.

He was coming hard and fast across the open ground as she fumbled shaking fingers on the gate closure. Couldn't get it to flip open.

Couldn't-get-damn-fingers-working.

The lock flipped up and she yanked the gate open.

Kyle grabbed her arm and hauled her back. She turned, kicking, scratching.

Something thudded on Kyle's back and sent them both stumbling. He screamed as he released her and she yanked away. Stumbled back through the gate and hauled it closed behind her. Fumbled the padlock from her pocket and into the hole in the lock.

In the pen, Kyle's flashlight lay on the dusty soil. Its light revealed Kyle struggling with a tawny, golden-eyed predator. The cougar had attacked him from behind, wrapping her huge paws and claws around his shoulders, her teeth at the back of his neck.

Kyle was screaming, batting at the animal, struggling to get the claws free of his chest. The front of his green t-shirt and jean jacket was already shiny with blood.

Cat stood frozen but then turned away.

Sy. She had to help Sy.

13

A scent of roses filled the worst part of Sy's dream. He was back on the hillside, forever pushing the incredibly heavy stone up the hill. The heat of Hades burned his flesh. The light was eternally either glaring bright or blackest night. His muscles strained against the burden and his back was breaking. All due to the ache in his head and his heart. Where once he thought he could do this forever if he had to—no God was going to make him regret his life—now there was no way he could continue this labor. At least not and remain sane. There—there were too many other things in existence. Too many other things that he wanted to do. One of them involved the heady scent of roses.

"Cat."

"Your girlfriend isn't here, lover boy. She abandoned you to my ministrations."

A rough palm slapped his cheek.

Where? Who?

"Cat?" he said. His voice sounded weak and cracked like a bad radio signal.

"Like I said. Not here."

Who was that? Where was he? His muscles didn't ache like

they had for half an eternity. He wasn't lying, crushed, on the hillside for letting the stone defeat him. He tried to pull his hand up to his face, but something restrained his wrists. He couldn't move.

He blinked open his eyes and found himself in darkness, but it was incomplete, unlike the hellish nights that Hades devised when unseen creatures nipped his heels as he fought that boulder up the hill.

The light came from a flashlight set on a table, its light splayed across a ceiling of rough beams and cobwebs that wavered in his vision. The ceiling was held up by dusty log walls and a window by the door was covered in tattered plastic…

He knew where he was.

He'd come to the cabin to wait for Cat's call for help. He went to scramble up from the chair he sat on, but his bonds stopped him. A woman's silhouette stepped from his side to in front of him.

"Well, lookit who's finally awake." Jana leered down at him. "I was beginning to think that I'd hit you too hard."

Hit him? He blinked as the memory came flooding in. Cat's cry and him heading out the door to answer, only to trip on a wire outside the door. When he'd come up from his sprawl on the ground, something had crashed into his head from behind. There was a spot on his skull that seriously throbbed.

"You hit me," he said, wincing as he tried to make his vision steady. How could it be Jana? Over the six years he'd known her, Jana had always been his friend.

"Well, give the man a gold star. Yes, I did, and it was a good hit, too. Right on the noggin. You went down like a cow in a slaughterhouse." She grinned down at him. "How do you like being low man on the totem pole for a change?"

He closed his eyes, trying to make sense of it all. Jana hit him? "Believe me when I say that I've been low man far longer than you'll ever know." He thought a moment. "Why hit me?"

Sighing, Jana hauled the other chair from the table to in front of him. She plunked down on it and scanned him up and down. "You know, I'm kinda sorry it came to this. I've almost liked working for you and watching you extricate yourself from all those romances I set you up for. But then you go and get yourself involved with exactly the wrong person—the one person my brother has a grudge to settle with."

Brother? "Kyle Redburn is your brother?" Oh, gods, no! And he'd encouraged Cat to bring Jana in on their plot to catch Kyle...

She grinned and shrugged. "Surprise?"

She shook her head almost as if the situation bothered her. "So it came down to this. I had to keep you from helping Cat so my brother could finish what he'd started. Simple, really. And if you're really good, you might just live through this."

She smiled and leaned in to pat his cheek, but the look in her eye was seriously off. He'd seen the same look in his own eyes before he'd died and spent eternity atoning for his hubris. This woman and her brother would do whatever it took to get what they wanted—revenge. He seriously doubted that his continued existence entered anywhere into their plans.

Jana stood and paced to the other side of the room. She sat down at the table. He tested his bonds. Surprisingly, his wrists could move inside the ropes on his wrists. Keeping an eye on Jana, he pulled his wrists apart and was surprised to feel the ends of the ropes slide past his wrists. No one tied ropes that badly, so he'd obviously had help. Cat must have been here and somehow escaped.

His gaze traveled up to the light reflecting on the tattered plastic at the window. The inside was a loose flap shoved back and the exterior was tattered shreds. He half-smiled to himself. Good on Cat. From being a woman who wouldn't step out of her house, she'd gone through a window like a hero.

That meant she was running for her life, could be fighting for her life, right now.

Jana was busy with a book she had illuminated by flashlight. He kept his upper body still so as not to alarm Jana and tested his ankle bonds. Also loosened. God bless Cat, for innumerable reasons.

He used his feet to rid himself of the ankle ropes and sat considering.

He had no weapon, but from what he'd seen, neither did Jana. She thought he was restrained in the chair. That meant the element of surprise was on his side *and* he was larger and stronger. The only weapon to hand was the chair he sat on. That meant Jana was going to have payback for the bump on his head. He just had to make sure that she didn't have time to yell for help. He didn't want to warn Kyle.

He rid his wrists of their bonds and readied himself.

One.

Two.

Three.

He launched himself across the room, the chair in his hands. Too late, Jana looked up from her reading. Her hand shifted to a gun on the table that had been hidden by her book. He brought the chair down on her head and shoulders.

She collapsed face-down on the table, then slithered to the floor. He checked her pulse. Strong and steady. Retrieving the ropes, he quickly tied her wrists and feet, and confiscating her flashlight and the gun, he headed out the door.

After the musty closeness of the cabin, the night air was cool and scented of leaves. The breeze rustled the branches over his head, but otherwise all was abnormally still. He kept the flashlight off because having his eyes adjust to darkness would serve him best. And he couldn't very well sneak up on Kyle Redburn with his flashlight advertising his presence.

He loped down the trail, careful of trip wires like the one that had taken him down at the cabin, old familiarity allowing him to traverse it with no problems. When he came to the bat shed, he stopped and stood listening. The night ached with silence as if the forest and its denizens held their breath. Overhead the trees sighed sympathy with the ocean wind, but there were no bats winging past, no owls soaring through the trees. Something was happening.

He edged around the bat shed and peered down the trail. The series of sheds and pens were staggered down the slope toward the admin building and its lone, amber, parking lot light. Inside the bat shed, all was silence. The bats were out feeding and doing their nightly sojourn. In the other sheds, the other animals were either sick, injured, or unable to be rehabilitated due to permanent injury. Most would spend the rest of their lives at the refuge.

He crept down the hill, wary of being seen. Kyle Redburn was somewhere near, he could feel it.

A human scream and the cougar's snarl cut through the night.

Sy forgot his caution and darted down the trail and between the buildings. There was the cougar pen gate. There was a trim figure outside the gate, leaning on the raptor shed for balance. Inside the cougar cage, a male figure struggled under the cougar's weight.

"Dammit!" Sy leapt into action.

He ran to Cat. "You okay?"

She nodded. He turned to the cage, unlocked the padlock, then pulled the gate open and stepped inside. He pulled the gate closed behind him.

Kyle had gone to his knees. The cougar tore at the back of his neck.

"Off!" Sy yelled and waved his arms.

The cat only lifted a bloody muzzle and snarled.

"Get off!" He stamped his feet, made himself as large as he

could, and advanced. He had the gun but would avoid using it at all costs.

Growling, the cat sat up and bared its teeth.

"Off!" Sy took a chance and leapt at the cougar.

The animal stood and backed off, snarling its fury. Kyle collapsed unconscious on the ground. Sy stayed where he was, waving his arms.

The cougar turned and slunk away.

Sy grabbed Kyle by the shoulders, but the man was too heavy.

"Cat, give me a hand," he called.

In a moment she was at his side, then picked up the comatose man's legs. Together they half carried and half dragged him out of the cougar pen, then dropped him on the ground.

Sy dropped to his knees beside Kyle. He pulled out the flashlight and ran the light over the man's wounds. The only thing that had protected Kyle was his denim jacket. And still his neck was torn and bloody. The shoulders of the jacket and the t-shirt and flesh beneath were all shredded from claws.

"We need to call an ambulance."

"We need to call the police," Cat said. The exhaustion and pain in her voice brought his head up.

She had braced herself against the cougar cage. The way her fingers strained in the chain link, it looked like only they held her upright. She held one leg gingerly off the ground.

And yet she'd been there to help him get Kyle out of the cage.

"I've got my cell in my pocket. At least I think it's still there." She let go of the fence with one hand and winced as she took more weight on both legs.

Sy was up off the ground in an instant and scooped her up. "What's happened to you?"

She grinned up at him. "Oh, well, I've done trail running in the dark. Tripped over a wire. Fallen down a ravine and twisted my ankle. Oh, and then there was the crowbar slamming me in the back…" She shrugged and did her best to look strong. "All in a day's work."

He hugged her to him, burying his face in her hair. "Thank the gods, you're safe. When I came to, I was terrified for you. Then I realized what you'd done for me…" He raised his face from the shadows of her hair and kissed her. Even through the mud and the tangle of cedar in her hair, she was still scented of roses. And he loved her.

It was an unexpected realization. One he didn't feel prepared for. Wasn't love only for fools and patsies? The kind of thing he'd always abhorred when he was king. Love might launch a thousand ships—for a foolish man, and he was no fool.

He settled Cat on her feet again, feeling badly when she winced, but said nothing.

"I better get this guy trussed up." He took Kyle's belt and used it on Kyle's arms. Sy used his own belt on Kyle's ankles. He glanced up at Cat when he was done. She was a slim, dark figure holding his flashlight, her features only half seen.

"You okay to keep an eye on this guy?" he asked. "And just so you know, his partner's out of the picture, too. I left Jana tied up in the cabin."

She nodded, so Sy left her to retrieve a wheelbarrow, then returned to find her leaned against the cage gate patiently waiting. He manhandled Kyle's limp form into the wheelbarrow to move him down to the admin building. They could call the police and ambulance from there—hopefully.

———

The flashlight sliced the night into vignette pieces for Cat. Darkness and Kyle Redburn comatose at her feet. Sy's strong back managing the top-heavy, loaded wheelbarrow away from the cage and around the corner headed to the administration building. The darkness of the area outside of the cage after Sy had left her to limp after him. The cool wind almost freezing her skin after the warmth of Sy's touch. The hush of the forest—normal, now, with the sound of life— which was strange given it seemed like her life was draining away.

She'd felt it happen with Sy. When he'd set her away, she'd felt the finality of the move. It was as if a door had shuttered closed and been barred. A great force had come between them and she'd felt the universe laughing. After all these years of having her life on hold, how could she expect that the first man she met would mean she'd retrieved herself?

Sy didn't need her. He had other labors to take care of. His animals, for example. They were his passion—not a silly reclusive woman. Sighing, she straightened and winced at the knife pain that cut through her knee. She must have really done something in her original fall and then aggravated it when she kept using it. Well, what was done, was done.

She trained the flashlight on the ground and followed after Sy, barely able to place her weight on her injured leg. The night swirled in a kaleidoscope of black and white and telescoped in until there was only the next footstep in front of her.

And then suddenly brilliance illuminated the forest. Sy must have turned on every light in the refuge. She made a visor from her hand to shield her eyes and kept going, finally hobbling through the front door of the admin building. The wheelbarrow stood in front of Jana's desk. Sy sat at the desk with the phone in his hand but glanced up when she pushed in.

"Hell and Hades," he said and lowered the phone. Then he brought it back to his face. "You better make that at least two ambulances. We've got at least two—possibly three injured." He nodded. "You've got the address then? Good. See you in a few minutes."

"The phones weren't working," she said from the doorway.

"There's a master switch. Jana had it turned off. She must have known it would be you trying to call for help."

He stood and came around the desk to her. "Dammit, Cat. I didn't realize." Gently he shoved her hair back from her brow. "You're bleeding."

She pulled away. She didn't need his sympathy. It was bad enough that she'd been stupid enough to fall for him. It would only hurt worse if she let him tend to her wounds.

"I'm fine. Really. It's only a flesh wound. I hope you didn't order an ambulance for me."

"You should sit down. You need to sit down." He caught her elbow and tried to lead her around the desk to Jana's chair.

She jerked away and almost fell, catching herself with her bad leg. The moan escaped before she could stop it and Sy scooped her up again and set her in the chair. Unlike before, this time he touched her as if it burned him.

Over. It was so over between them and she had to get over him. She bowed her head to compose herself.

When she looked up, she found Sy watching her.

"Cat, listen."

She held up her hand. "You've got nothing you need to say to me. It has been a good time and you've gone through hell and back to help me. Thank you. I might even get my life back now. Shoot, I can even go back to probation work if I want." And face down the defense lawyers who would oppose her reports to the court claiming they were biased by her victimization.

He looked like he was choosing his words when a groan from Kyle brought them both around to the wheelbarrow.

Kyle Redburn glared at her and for once it didn't send a terrified shiver down her spine.

"It's over, Kyle. Another assault on me. Attempted murder, even. This time it'll be remand in custody and then a jail sentence. You won't see the outside for a very long time."

He grinned the terrifying crooked grin she remembered, his

teeth gleaming yellow in the fluorescent lighting so they seemed to match the tawny log walls of the building.

"No longer than you, kitty-cat. You're a house-cat now and I did that."

God, the twisted mind of this man who preferred to gloat over what he'd taken from her rather than accept responsibility for what he'd done. It was exhausting to think about. And there were so many others like him. Maybe not quite as twisted, maybe not twisted enough to attack their probation officer, but twisted enough that they'd hurt more people. The thought of working with those men and women again was simply exhausting. She closed her eyes and leaned her head back against the chair's headrest. "You keep on thinking that, Kyle. You'll be gone and you'll never know what I'm doing, but if it helps you, go ahead and think you've won."

She opened her eyes and leaned toward him. "But remember this: I was here at the refuge tonight, and I escaped you twice on my own. I don't need four walls to protect me anymore. I—I'm free now." And as she said it, she meant it, even though part of that freedom was her heart hurting just a little too much.

The morning was bright with sunlight and the glorious brilliance of Cat's next-door neighbor's dahlias. The large blooms nodded their yellow, red, and purple heads in the light ocean breeze that coasted over Cat's skin as she watched Elizabeth Whitcombe, her next-door neighbor, prune back her roses in quick, efficient movements that Cat was trying desperately to follow. Just how did the woman know where to cut?

"You see, dear?" Mrs. Whitcombe asked, looking up with her vivid blue gaze from under the broad brim of her straw hat. She was a willowy woman of long gray hair that she tied up in a chignon under her hat. She wore a pale-blue, long-sleeved cotton shirt and long, tan, flowing trousers. A faded scarf of tan and blue was tied around the crown of her hat and lifted slightly in the breeze.

"I—I think so," Cat nodded. "You cut just above the branching to encourage the bush to get fuller."

"That's right, dear." Mrs. Whitcomb straightened and eased her back. She wore plain white gloves on her hands and had admitted to Cat that she covered up "because of a little skin cancer scare." But she loved to garden and so she was back, just with more protection.

Cat felt a lot like that. It had been two weeks since Kyle Redburn was arrested and she ceased worrying about looking over her shoulder all the time. She once more reveled in her independence. She'd even mended things with Jude and had spent a weekend with her friend in Vancouver. In celebration she had gone to a local nursery and had bought the flowers that charmed her in order to redo her garden. Sy would like it, she had thought. She sighed. The garden was supposed to be something to keep her mind off other things. When she'd brought the plants home, Mrs. Whitcomb had come to the rescue when Cat found herself overwhelmed with trying to decide where to plant her floral treasures. Since then, they had become fast friends.

"You're looking far away, dear. Penny for your thoughts."

She came back to herself from thoughts of the floral perfume wafting into her bedroom while Sy and she made love. It wasn't going to happen. It couldn't happen because Sy had made it very clear what he thought. She sighed again.

"All right. That's it." Gentle Mrs. Whitcomb crossed her arms over her chest. "This has gone on long enough. You've been mooning about and sighing for days now as if your best friend died. I thought you wanted to know about the flowers and the garden, but I'm beginning to think that you're using me as a distraction." The old woman's mouth made a little moue as she stared down Cat's intended denial.

Finally, Cat sighed again and nodded. "Maybe. A little. I'm sorry. I do want to learn, but I know I'm distracted."

Mrs. Whitcomb gave her the once over. "Let me guess. It was the nice young man who was visiting quite frequently for a while. The tall one with dark hair."

Girding herself for the grilling to come, Cat nodded again. "We had a bit of a thing, but then he basically ended it the night the guy who was stalking me was arrested. I guess I was simply too high maintenance."

Regardless of no longer being trapped in her home, she had too much baggage for any normal guy. Not that she'd ever think of Sy as normal. The guy was terrific. Any woman would be lucky.

The lump that had been plaguing her stomach and throat rose a little higher. Seeing Sy with whoever was the next lucky girl was going to be plenty hard. It was why she hadn't been back to the refuge—it might break her heart, and she was feeling mighty fragile at the moment.

She met Mrs. Whitcomb's kindly gaze. "If you don't mind, I think I'd rather not talk about it."

Disbelief flared briefly in Mrs. Whitcomb's gaze, but was quickly masked. She nodded. "I suppose that might be best. The man is obviously flawed given he hasn't come looking for you. You don't need that kind of fool in your life. He must be far too full of himself—think he's too important or something."

"Or something." But that wasn't Sy at all. He'd been kind, loving. He'd risked grave harm to himself in order to help her. He'd been funny, and the dedication to his animals had been almost…heroic was the word that came to mind.

And he didn't want her in his life.

"It's most likely as you say—for the better. I don't need the headaches of a man in my life. All that compromise. I'd rather do things my way."

And yet she kept looking at the blackberry brambles in the back of her yard and thinking that she'd really like Sy's opinion on whether she should clear them away. The fact that they were a natural shelter for her animal neighbors sort of charmed her. Should she keep them for the animals—something she figured Sy would do—or clear them away as Jude had suggested to improve the value of her property. Not that she was thinking about selling or anything.

"Now that I can leave the house, it's time for me to get back to work. Thing is, I'm not sure that I can go back to probation work. My heart isn't in it. To do that job, you have to have a lot more confidence that what you're doing is right. I'm not so sure anymore. Are we too hard on people or too lenient? Why do we treat our cases differently? It's because we're all fallible, or some would call it gullible. We want to believe what our clients tell us."

Cat sank down on her heels feeling suddenly exhausted. "The trouble is, probation is all I'm trained to do. A criminology degree isn't much good to a lot of people." She rubbed her dirty hand over her face and was pretty sure that she hadn't made things better when Mrs. Whitcomb's moue deepened. "Any ideas what a washed-up probation officer can do to make herself useful on the Sunshine Coast?"

Nodding, Mrs. Whitcomb turned back to the flowers, then stopped and handed Cat the pruning shears, insisting when Cat wanted to refuse. Finally, Cat dragged up to standing again, this time taking her chances pruning the older woman's roses.

Cat tentatively made a cut, the young end of a branch falling sadly to the earth.

"That's a better attitude, at least. Out with the old, in with the new. If your fellow hasn't the brains to see what's in you, then you don't want him." From down the hill came the rumble of vehicles on the highway.

Cat nodded, but the trouble was, she really did. Sy filled her nights and she found herself daydreaming about him—thus the trip to the nursery.

"Earth to Cat. Earth to Cat. You're gone again."

A vehicle engine revved as it started up the hill. Cat glanced at the woman and found her own eyes tearing. Jeezus God, she was not a soppy woman who got devastated by breakups. She was better than this.

But the darn lump was now firmly embedded in her throat and she simply couldn't catch her breath.

"Oh, honey." Mrs. Whitcomb's warm arms came around her and Cat inhaled her scent of flowers, spring, and amber. For such a tiny woman, Mrs. Whitcomb's arms were strong and Cat couldn't help herself. The lump dissolved into tears that just wouldn't stop falling. She was a blubbering fool.

Mrs. Whitcomb's warm arms and her "there-theres" were more comfort than Cat had expected.

———

S y accelerated his Ford truck up the hillside, the pine and cedars flashing blinding sunlight and shadows through the truck's streaked windscreen. He needed to wash the truck. The inside was even worse—a mess of fast food wrappers and newspapers that leaked the scents of ink, old ketchup, and grease into the air. Only the gaily colored bouquet of lilies, daisies, and freesia helped mask it. He'd never let his truck get this bad before. In fact, he'd always kept it pristine—but these last few weeks he couldn't seem to get his act together.

The sun was hot through the windows, the air conditioning barely keeping up. The unforgivingly empty blue sky seemed to go on forever beyond the treetops, and the houses he passed seemed like so many empty boxes. Even the gardens that seemed painted on the yards appeared faded and wilted, as if there was very little will to live in this world.

That had to be exhaustion talking. These past two weeks had been unforgivingly busy. First there'd been the frantic efforts to stop Conservation officers from destroying the cougar. They had every right to do so after she attacked a human, but he'd made his case about the circumstances of Kyle Redburn entering the cage to attack Cat and the fact that Cat had hidden in the cage for a time with no trouble. Surprisingly, the Conservation officers had agreed that the big cat could live—provided she was released deep in the mountains. He'd spent the past few days arranging just such a release. The cat would be taken up abandoned logging roads deep into Carron Park.

That was one success he could be proud of.

Good thing, because the rest of his life felt like it was falling apart. He'd never realized how much he depended upon Jana at the refuge, and trying to schedule volunteers to fill her shoes was plain madness. He'd hired a girl from the local veterinary practice to fill in a few days a week, but that left him tied to administration five days out of seven when there were other things he needed to take care of.

And then there was the fact that he wasn't sleeping.

He scrubbed at his newly shaved chin. For the past few days he'd been sporting a beard because self-care really didn't fit into his schedule. He'd even found his last laundered shirt to wear for this occasion, though his jeans had seen a few days of wear in the cages. It couldn't be helped.

Last night he'd spent the night at the refuge because a doe deer had been brought in with a broken leg. She'd been placed in a sling to make sure she put no weight on the leg, and he was making sure that she didn't panic and get tangled in the sling. It had been a long night for contemplation, catching shut-eye on a cot placed on the far side of the doe's stall. Contemplation and too many powerful memories.

Memories of the mountain and the boulder had been particularly strong. This morning his muscles ached from the remembered labor. And all the time the memory—or perhaps it was a dream—had placed Cat Moore at the top of the mountain. Something to strive for, but he never seemed to reach the top of the mountain. By the end of the night, he was ready to roar his frustration into the hellish dawn of his nightmares.

He'd woken to find the deer slumbering in the sling and, strangely, the scent of roses lingering. From where, he didn't know, because Cat Moore had been nowhere near the refuge since the ambulance had taken her away that awful night.

She probably couldn't stand to see him, which made his current mission feel a little more futile. His stomach felt like a stone and his flipping palms were sweaty on the steering wheel. He felt like—like—dammit he didn't know what this was like, but it felt foolish and as if he should turn the truck around and head back to the refuge. He was a proud man. He'd been a king. He didn't need this.

But he was a king no longer. He'd labored longer and more lowly than any man in history. Hades and Persephone had done that to him.

And the awful truth was that he sorely missed Cat Moore with her bright cap of hair, her dark thoughtful eyes, and her vivid smile. He liked her strength and her bravery and her smarts and, well, pretty much everything about her. He wanted her with him, not as something owned, a possession, like he had in the past. He wanted something more. Something that would remove the boulder in his gut and in his past.

He turned onto the residential street and spotted the two women in the garden as he neared the house. Swallowing back the cowardly urge to simply drive past, he eased into the curb and parked. Then, taking a deep breath of the grease and floral scent, he climbed out of the truck with the bouquet. It was only then that he allowed himself to look back at the two women.

Cat and the elderly female gardener he'd spoken to before. The old woman wore the same shroud of loose-fitting clothing she'd worn the other day. Cat, on the other hand, looked fresh as a new penny in white Bermuda shorts and a sleeveless black-and-white polka dot blouse. Both women wore gardening gloves and Cat had an artful smudge of dirt on her left cheek.

"Hey," he tried. It was the only thing he could think of to say that wouldn't result in him spilling his feelings out like a madman.

He struck out, picking his way through the wildly verdant garden toward them. Cat stayed where she was, her expression unreadable.

Was he an idiot for doing this or an idiot for staying away so long?

He came up to her and held out the bouquet. "For you."

Her gaze was huge and liquid as she accepted the flowers. "They're beautiful. Thank you. But why give them to me?"

"Yes, why?" the older woman said softly.

"Because I saw them and thought of you," he said, feeling awkward. "I mean, I was thinking of you, and then I saw the flowers and I knew they were for you and I was thinking of you more and knew I had to bring them to you."

Aah, damn. He sounded like a complete fool.

He closed his eyes and inhaled. "Let me try this again. I've been thinking. A lot. About you. About us. I was an idiot the other night. My only excuse is the feelings were pretty much more than I was used to. I—I wondered if there was a chance of us trying again."

Cat was so still that he was positive she was going to turn him down. The old woman looked as if she was holding her breath just like he was.

"You mean you want to be part of my life?" Her voice was soft and almost wondering.

He nodded. "I've realized that the few weeks with you were the most memorable years I've had in a very long time. I've realized that you mean more to me than anything and I want the chance to see whether we can make things work. Will you take that chance? Can you?"

Cat seemed to consider. Her gaze was serious as if she was assessing all his faults. Then her pink lips curved into a mischievous smile.

"I think I might be willing to do that!"

Suddenly his arms were full of warm woman and the sun no

longer seemed to glare, the garden hummed with bees, and the scent of roses was all around him so he was almost drunk.

Beyond Cat's shoulder and the silken strands of her hair, the old woman's shape seemed to come apart for a moment and reform into the tall, striking figure he had last seen on Hades' mountain. Persephone looked down at him and smiled and then her form came apart into a million golden butterflies that danced over the garden around them until they lifted into the sky. Behind her, she left only an old woman swathed in linens, a broad straw hat, and gardening gloves.

Cat looked up then, at the swirl of wings and then down at him with her dark gaze dancing. "Amazing."

He leaned down and drank in her scent before tasting her lips.

"You have no idea," he said.

If you enjoyed *Dangerous Haven*, you might enjoy *Surviving Safe Harbour*. Turn the page to read the opening chapter.

SURVIVING SAFE HARBOR

Ronnie Baxter sat with her knees pulled up to her chest on a life jacket cabinet on the forward viewing deck of the massive ferry. The wind tangled in her long hair. The deck throbbed with the engines, but the vibrant air was filled with salt brine and gull cries—so different from the cloying landlocked life she'd lived for so long. It was almost like coming back to life again—if she could quit looking over her shoulder.

Her four-year-old daughter Maddy—short for Madeline—sat beside her in her favorite pink hoodie and leggings, holding up pieces of her sandwich for the gulls. It was a pretty sight. Maddy's hair, a shade blonder than Ronnie's strawberry blonde, streamed against the pink of her clothing. The green of the rugged B.C. coastal mountains and the blue of sea and sky served as backdrop.

Under the warmth of the sun, watching the joyous way that white-winged gulls slipped through the air, Ronnie almost believed that there was a future for the two of them. That they'd finally left behind all the darkness.

A gust of wind chilled Ronnie. Maddy let the last bit of her sandwich fall to the deck.

"It's cold, Mommy." She cuddled into Ronnie's side and a single gull showed bravado, swooped and scooped up the fallen bread only to be attacked by the other gulls for a piece of his bounty. They flew off screaming.

Ronnie inhaled Maddy's baby shampoo scent and shivered.

"Why are they doing that, Mommy? That one seagull was brave and got the bread all by himself?"

Ronnie hugged her daughter a little closer. "Some people think you should always share, sweetie."

At least, shared custody was what the judges and lawyers had said, regardless of all the proof of spousal abuse. They couldn't or wouldn't believe that there were already signs that the violence was spreading to Maddy, and that was a potentiality Ronnie couldn't allow to develop.

She kissed Maddy's soft hair. "Next time we'll have to remember to bring more bread. You remind me, 'kay?"

Maddy nodded.

The massive car ferry chugged around the string of islands that filled the entrance to Howe Sound. Ahead, by the water at the base of a mountain, was what looked like a tangled scaffolding. "Look. There's where we're going." She pointed.

"And where's our house going to be?"

Where indeed. Ronnie checked over her shoulder. "We have to find a house, sweetie. We're going to have an adventure and camp for a little while."

Until she could find daycare and a job that could pay for everything. After all the lawyer's bills from fighting her husband's demands, she didn't really have—in her dead father's words—the proverbial pot to pee in or the window to throw it out of. The world felt very lonely.

The ship's engines changed rhythm and Ronnie stood. "I think we better head down to the car."

Maddy jumped down beside her and headed for the rail, Ronnie hovering behind her. The high decks made her nervous—

not that the decks didn't have plenty of rails, but four-year-olds had a knack for finding ways through boundaries. Just like Maddy had burst full-blown into Ronnie's heart the moment she'd realized she was pregnant. It might not have been a planned pregnancy—something that had infuriated Jared, something he'd demanded she end—but it was still the best thing that had ever happened to Ronnie. Even if it had marked the beginning of the end for her marriage.

No way was she letting her little girl be raised by a violent man.

"Look, Mommy! There's a man in the water!" Madeline's young voice carried and caught the attention of other passengers.

"Where, honey? Where?" Because a man in the ocean had about ten minutes to get himself out before the cold and the waves took him. She at least remembered that from her time as a kayak guide years ago. Before marriage had turned her timid.

Maddy was pressed up against the rail pointing down into the water.

Ronnie followed the length of the chubby little-girl arm and saw…

Waves. A light chop. No sign of a boat or kayak. A swimmer? But it was an awfully long way from shore and no swimmer in their right mind would swim right into the ferry's route.

A shadow passed under the waves as if there was something there. Then a head bobbed up in the water and looked up at her. Dark, intelligent eyes met hers. An aquiline nose and wide mouth and then something happened—a shimmer of light on water—and there was a gray, furred head and black nose.

Ronnie stumbled back from the rail. What had she just seen?

"It's just a seal," said a young man with a backpack who had joined them. "No person'd be stupid enough to swim out this far in the ocean."

Maddy frowned. "But it was a man. I saw a man." She looked confidently up at the backpacker.

"It couldn't have been a man, sweetie. Look." Ronnie pointed back at the waves as the seal rolled in the water exposing speckled gray-and-black hide before he dove. "That's a seal. People don't have spots like that."

Maddy shook her head. "I saw a man."

"Isn't that sweet. She's so sure. You are a sharp-eyed little one," cooed a grandmotherly type with the steel gray eyes of a jail guard. "She really is a sweet one," the woman said, looking at Ronnie.

Getting the once over from someone—a few someones, given Maddy's cry had brought a number of people to the rail— wasn't exactly the way to remain anonymous.

She couldn't afford to be memorable. Ronnie caught Maddy's hand and tugged her back from the rail. "She has a vivid imagination. Come on, sweetie."

She hauled Maddy after her, through the door into the ferry and out of the wind, then down the many stairs to the rumble and engine noise of the car decks. She keyed them into the ancient Civic hatchback and collapsed into her seat in the comforting scent of old fast food wrappers and yogurt tubes. Their lone suitcase sat in the hatch amid sleeping bags, toys, and Maddy's favorite teddy bear.

Ronnie's heart was pounding. So were her ears. She inhaled and closed her eyes. There was too good a chance that Jared would figure out what she'd done instead of going to Disneyworld as she'd announced. With her arrival back in Chicago long past due, Jared would be looking for them. So would the authorities. And with her dual citizenship, it wasn't hard to figure out that she might run back to her mother's home country. The fact that she had never been to the west coast was her one hope. Jared would figure she'd go to a place where people she knew could help her. But there was still the potential for her or Maddy's face to be publicized in the media. They couldn't afford to be memorable.

"Mommy? Are you all right?"

Ronnie opened her eyes and winked in the rearview mirror at her daughter in her child's seat.

"Never better," she said, mimicking the British accent of the actress in her daughter's favorite wizarding movie.

Maddy's grin wiped out the concern that had placed a little line between her eyes. "Never better, indeed."

It was a favorite game between them.

The ferry engines slowed and loudspeakers announced that it was time for passengers to return to their vehicles. Through the open windows on the car deck waited the forested folds of the mountains, the rocky shorelines, and the small towns of a place optimistically called the Sunshine Coast.

§

Three days later, and still tasting the remains of yet another lunchtime peanut butter sandwich, Ronnie sat on a towel at the beach at the Roberts Creek Campground and counted what remained of her cash one more time. Maddy played in the ocean fifteen feet away. A piddling three hundred Canadian dollars and change, and the campsite was costing her twenty dollars a night. She had to find a job—there was only so long they could survive on peanut butter and jelly—but so far her ventures into the Roberts Creek businesses and even into Sechelt, the larger town farther north, hadn't landed her a job that could pay for rent or even pay for her current bills. Heaven knew she needed to get herself and Maddy settled before school started if they were going to make a go of it here. The trouble was, living in a campground didn't exactly put you in touch with the locals who might know of a job, and all of the local restaurants, shops, and grocery stores seemed to have filled their quota of summer employees—or if they hadn't filled them, they were only interested in hiring locals.

She stuffed her wallet back in her shorts and hugged her tanned knees anxiously while Maddy explored the small tidal pools along the shore. The sky was a perfect blue with puffy white clouds. Her daughter was the perfect blonde-haired child with natural ringlets down her back that caught the wind, her favorite orange bathing suit a natural foil against the blue backdrop. The forest rolled down to the crescent of beach, scenting the briny air with cedar. A perfect paradise for those who could afford it—made more picturesque by the phalanx of brightly colored kayaks rounding the point of the cove. The kayakers at the front and rear of the group had the easy even strokes of experienced paddlers. The middle eight did not—too much splashing, too high an angle for the paddles or the paddles barely touching the water.

A tour, then. That was the usual formation she'd used with a group of inexperienced paddlers long ago when she'd still been single and before the rest of her life had happened. Watching the paddlers across the water, she felt the ghostly pull and release of the muscles across her shoulders and back and settled back on the towel, her legs out before her just as they'd been in a kayak. Funny how the body remembered.

The group of kayaks came into shore. The leader deftly leaped out of his boat and hauled it up the beach before rushing back to catch each of his charges as they came into shore. Tall and tanned, eyes and dark hair shielded beneath sunglasses and a ball cap, she couldn't say what his face looked like, but the rest of him was deserving of a second or even third look. Typical summer employee looking to buff up his tan and his flirting among the female tourists. The kayaking companies back home had been full of that type—seasonal drifters who spent the winters bumming on the ski hills.

But there was nothing the matter with looking, was there? Strong shoulders with the roped muscle of the athlete who carried very little extra fat. Developed biceps and triceps from all that paddling, and a tattoo she couldn't quite make out on his left arm. Long swimmer's legs and large hands and feet. She hauled her study away, too aware of the old saying of what went along with large hands and feet. It had been three months since she left Jared, and while looking didn't hurt, there was no way she was getting involved again.

When she looked up again, those aviator sunglasses were tipped in her direction and she felt herself color as if he'd heard what she'd been thinking. She was pretty sure the eyes behind the glasses were assessing her faded cutoffs and worn, sleeveless t-shirt and finding her wanting.

She leapt up and strode over to Maddy. "So what are you discovering?"

"There are little crabs and clam shells!" Maddy proudly held up her bounty, then looked past Ronnie. "So are those the kind of kayaks you used to have, Mommy?"

Ronnie turned beside her. "Well, yes. They sort of are. Except Mommy's kayak was the color of the sky."

"Pretty," Maddy said.

"It was." But then Ronnie realized Maddy wasn't talking about the blue kayak lost in the sea of time. She was eyeing the rainbow of kayaks now brought up into a neat line on shore, while the paddlers gathered not too far from Ronnie's towel and were sharing around bags of carrots, packages of hummus, slabs of pita bread, and packages of sandwiches. The scent of ham and mustard, and tuna and cheese wafted over the cove.

"It smells good," Maddy said, just a little too loud.

It did. Ronnie's mouth watered far more than it ever would again over peanut butter and jelly. "It does smell good, but we just had our lunch. Remember?"

Maddy sighed and looked up at Ronnie with too-weary eyes. "Mommy, I'm really tired of peanut butter and jelly. Can we have something else tonight? I really like tuna sandwiches."

"Hey! If you like tuna, you're welcome to one of mine. I

have them all the time." The deep voice reminded Ronnie a little of waves hitting a rocky shoreline and the gentle spray that would mist up and cover your skin. She shivered.

Of course the speaker was none other than aviator sunglass boy. He stood up from his perch on a driftwood log and sauntered over, a neatly wax-paper-wrapped sandwich in his hand. "Here you go. If I do say so myself, it's a good tuna sandwich. A secret recipe—one of my specialties."

Maddy hesitated, awaiting Ronnie's approval. There was something about the guy. Something familiar, and yet he was about as different as possible from the guys Ronnie knew. By the squint lines edging out of the sunglasses, he was older than she'd first thought, too. Thirty-six or-seven—a few years older than her. It was weird the way a place low down in her belly tingled pleasantly just standing beside him. But she was staying low profile, remember?

"This really isn't necessary. I can make my daughter a tuna sandwich."

The proffered sandwich lowered a little, but the wide mouth stretched in a grin that revealed even, white, male-supermodel teeth. "I'm sure you can, but your daughter seemed to have a hankering right now and I happen to have an extra sandwich."

He shifted the sandwich into his other hand and held out his hand in greeting. "Seth Cullen."

Ronnie hesitated but then accepted his grip—firm, callused, so this wasn't just some pretty boy. "Ronnie Baxter. This is Maddy, my daughter."

"Well how do you do, Maddy? You know, you really could help me out by taking my sandwich. I always make too many of them and then I have to eat them myself. If I don't eat them, they go bad, you know." There was just the slightest of lilt in his voice that made Ronnie think of Gaelic songs, fishing boats, and fiddles, but then the accent faded as if he was tucking that part of him away. For all he was a tour leader and in the public eye every day, this man carried secrets with him.

She didn't trust secrets—not that she didn't have them herself.

But Maddy gravely accepted the crisply-wrapped sandwich. "Thank you. I'm sure I will enjoy it."

Lord, she sounded about fifty, not four, but living through a violent home life could age a child the same as the mother.

"That was politely said," Seth said.

"I've tried to raise her right." Ronnie leaned down to her daughter. "Why don't you go sit on our towel and eat your sandwich. That way you can tell Mr. Cullen how much you've enjoyed it."

Maddy scampered off and Ronnie looked up at Seth Cullen. He really was tall. And decidedly good looking even though she couldn't see his eyes behind his sunglasses. Better yet, he wasn't one of those guys who seemed to know it and revel in the fact that every woman around was noticing. He wore an old, sleeveless t-shirt, its red so faded it was almost pink. On the front, also faded, was an emblem of a coastline with the words Coastal Kayak encircling the coastline. Encircling his right bicep, the tattoo revealed itself to be a seal twined with either a piece of translucent green seaweed or a scarf. It was amazing the way the artist had caught the light in the fabric.

"I take it you're a tour leader," Ronnie said, to break the uncomfortable silence.

"Yup. Something to do every summer. I bring groups out on day and overnight trips."

"Nice boats. All fiberglass. Usually companies just use plastic for their hires."

He nodded. "Plastic's sturdier and takes more abuse, but they don't have as much resale value."

"I remember. But these are either new or you've kept them in darn good condition."

He shrugged. "This is their second year, but I'm pretty careful what beaches we come to. And I threaten the rentals with physical harm if they hurt the boats." He leaned in and stage whispered the latter and then chuckled. "You seem to know about kayaks."

Ronnie shrugged. "It was a long time ago, in another life. I led tours myself. It was on the east coast. I haven't been in a kayak since, but I still remember it fondly." More than fondly, actually. She'd once tried to get Jared out in a kayak because Chicago wasn't exactly without access to shoreline, but it 'hadn't been his thing' and so she'd been told in no uncertain terms that she was expected to not have it be her thing either. That was when they were engaged, when Jared was still weaning her away from her friends. Before things turned bad.

She shivered and came to herself standing on a patch of sand in the west coast sunshine that had suddenly faded to cool. Seth Cullen looked down at her. Even at five-foot-seven beside him she felt small and she stumbled back a step. She wasn't going to let herself feel vulnerable anymore.

"Just where were you?" he asked, catching her elbow to steady her. His touch set a warm tingle right down to her core, and even with his eyes hidden, his expression was concerned.

She shook her head and tugged loose. "Nowhere that matters. Thinking about kayaks."

His mouth downturned. "It didn't look anyplace good. What, a kayak bite you sometime?"

She laughed and the dark memories passed. "No bites. One or two dunkings way back at the beginning. Nope. Kayaks were only a good thing."

His expression then turned calculating and he stepped in close and lowered his voice. "Listen. I've got to get this crew moving because they clearly are going to struggle going home against the current, but if you ever want to go out, why don't you give me a call. And if you're here for a while and interested in making a couple of dollars, maybe you'd be interested in helping out with the boats. We don't pay a lot, but it gets you out in the sunshine." He dug in a pocket of his baggy shorts and fished out a laminated business card with a non-faded version of the logo on his t-shirt.

She hesitated, but took it even though she knew she'd never use it. Seth Cullen, aka aviator shade guy, was a mite too attractive and she had no room in her life for that.

After thanking him for the card and the sandwich, she retreated to Maddy, who was busily vacuuming the sandwich down, all but the crusts—as usual.

"You know that all the best stuff is in the crusts, right?" she said as she settled beside her daughter.

"Never better, I know, but I thought that you like them so much, I'd save them for you, Mommy." Such an angelic face, before she broke into a gap-toothed grin.

"Never better, sly girl," Ronnie said and pulled Maddy into her side for a tickle before filching one of the crusts to chew on. It was—wonderful. The sweet-salt taste of tuna and relish and mayo tanging the bread was even better than she remembered. And totally beyond the budget of a woman trying to stretch a finite few dollars into an infinite future.

Seth Cullen and his assistant guide were busy settling their charges into their kayaks and shoving them back into the emerald-green cove. When the group was loaded, Seth shoved his boat into the waves and lightly slipped aboard as if he was made for the water. He raised a hand in her direction and then used his paddle to dragonfly across the water to lead his hesitant charges back around the headland. She liked the way his back muscles worked smoothly under his skin, almost as if man and kayak were one and the same.

Ronnie looked down at the business card and chewed another crust of tuna-infused bread. Seth Cullen was an attractive guy— not her type, because she was more into blonds—but there was something about him. Something that set a tingle in her skin that left her sorely tempted to call him. Thank God the last few years had taught her never to trust her feelings. 'If she ever wanted to go out,' indeed!

She flicked the card between her fingers. Seth Cullen. Had he actually been offering the chance for a job, or had he just been flirting?

To read more of Surviving Safe Harbor, check out
https://bookstoread.com/u/3L9g50

TO MY READERS

1. Thank you for reading *Dangerous Haven*. I hope you enjoyed it. If you did (and even if you didn't), it would be immensely helpful if you would leave a review. Reviews help other readers find this book.
2. Sign up for my Newsletter, and receive three free novels. To get your FREE eBOOKS, click HERE.
3. Check out my website for information on my books and extra content.
4. For more links and offers, or to chat with me, check out Facebook.

ABOUT THE AUTHOR

Karen L. Abrahamson writes fantasy, romance, and mysteries as Karen L. Abrahamson and K.L. Abrahamson. Her best known romance are the Unlocking Series in which a dangerous charmed bracelet comes into the lives of six friends in a sunny resort town. Her romantic suspense and mysteries take readers on adventures to dangerous locations around the world.

Her fantasy books include the unique Cartographer series in which secret agents of the American Geological Society use their powers to take on the purveyors of dark magic.

Karen lives on the Canadian west coast with bald eagles, bears and orcas for neighbours.

To find out more about her, her travels and her writing, visit www.karenlabrahamson.com

ROMANCE BY KAREN L. ABRAHAMSON

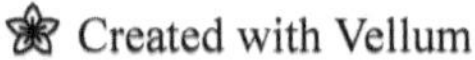 Created with Vellum